BESTIARIUM GREENLANDICA

Library and Archives Canada Cataloguing in Publication

Title: Bestiarium Greenlandica : a compendium of the mythical creatures, spirits, and strange beings of Greenland / edt. by Maria Bach Kreutzmann; translated by Charlotte Barslund.
Other titles: Bestiarium Groenlandica. English
Names: Kreutzmann, Maria Bach, editor. | Barslund, Charlotte, translator.
Description: Translation of: Bestiarium Groenlandica. | Includes bibliographical references and index.
Identifiers: Canadiana 20210263571 | ISBN 9781777081706 (hardcover)
Subjects: LCSH: Mythology, Greenlandic. | LCSH: Inuit mythology—Greenland. | LCSH: Folklore—
Greenland. | LCSH: Inuit—Greenland—Folklore. | LCSH: Animals—Folklore. | LCSH: Shamans—Greenland.
Classification: LCC GR214 .B4713 2021 | DDC 398.20998/2045—dc23

BESTIARIUM GREENLANDICA

A COMPENDIUM OF THE MYTHICAL CREATURES, SPIRITS, AND STRANGE BEINGS OF GREENLAND

Edited by Maria Bach Kreutzmann
Translated by Charlotte Barslund

www.eyeofnewtpress.com

I would like to thank everyone who has helped me,
supported me, guided me, and carried me.
A special thank you to my artists and researchers, without
whom this book could not have happened.
And a very big thank you to milik publishing for believing
in this book, especially to Julie Rehhoff Kondrup
for seeing it through from start to finish.

Maria Bach Kreutzmann

In honour of my ancestors and everyone I love

CONTENTS

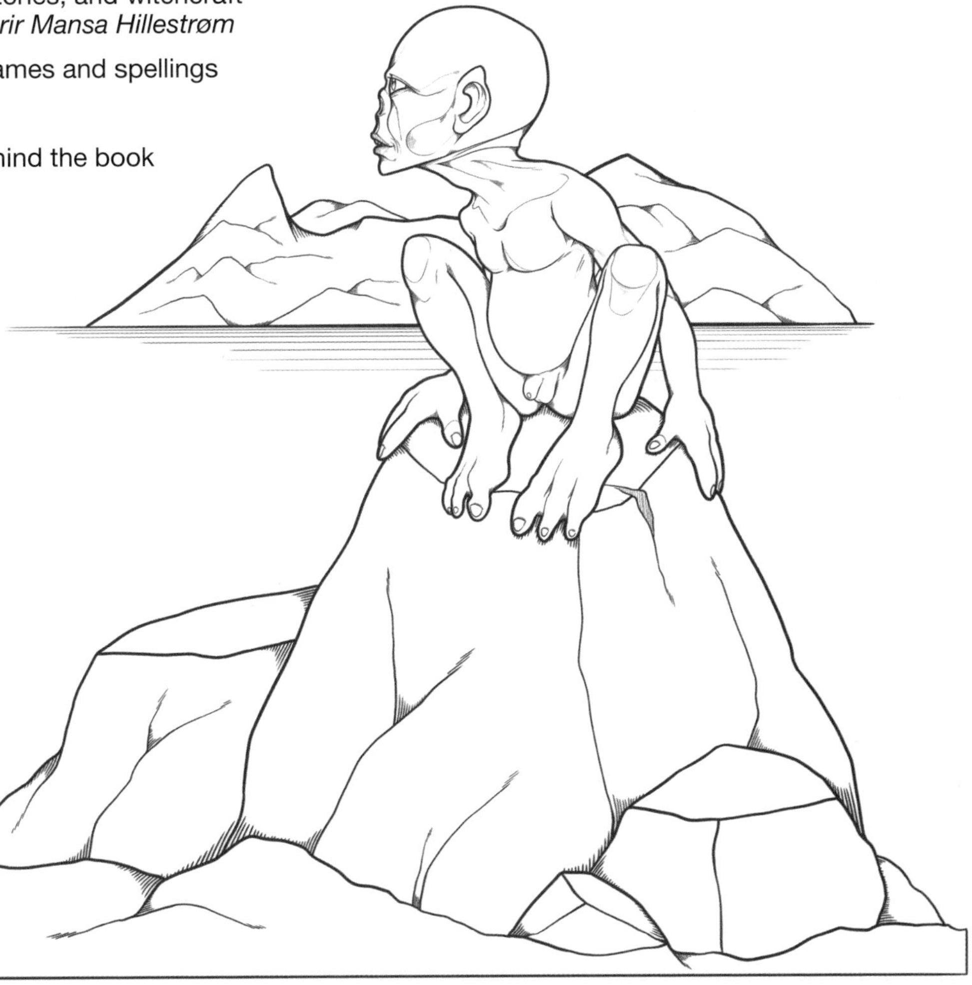

DEAR READER,

Five years ago, I was reading some old Greenlandic stories when I came across mythological creatures I didn't recognize. I was intrigued, and it prompted me to start looking out for other mythological creatures in my heritage. In time my hobby turned into a passion when I realized that I had grown up knowing only a fraction of them. The more I discovered, the more I began to appreciate the vastness of our world of old spirits and creatures. Whenever I asked other people here in Greenland, they, too, could usually name only a handful, but they were always delighted when I told them that the number of mystical creatures was much higher. I became attracted to the idea of examining and mapping all the creatures that live in our stories. This has now become a reality with this book.

When I moved back to Nuuk, I hired a team of skilled researchers as well as seven brilliant artists from Greenland, Iceland, and Denmark. I chose to work with a range of artists to see how their different styles and cultural backgrounds would influence the illustrations. Some artists already knew the creatures they would be drawing; others didn't. It has been a pleasure to help spread our culture and our stories to people outside of Greenland, which is another aim of this book. It is for all of us, all of them, and all of you, who will be the future cultural ambassadors for our country.

I am aware that not every story has been written down. We are the descendants of an oral narrative tradition. The older generation is an inexhaustible source of stories, and their knowledge of the world, which at times has been hidden and forgotten, should not be underestimated. It was they and their ancestors who told the stories to curious travellers and fellow Greenlanders, who then chose to write them down. Without these past collectors and our ancestors' stories, we would not have been able to describe these creatures or compile this book. My own family and my ancestors have also helped pass on our culture and cultural history over the last few centuries, and they have been in my thoughts, sitting on my shoulders, reminding me of the rich heritage that belongs to all of us—and which we must preserve through renewal.

How to read this book

The Latin, and first edition title *Bestiarium Groenlandica* was inspired by the scientific tradition of collecting and cataloguing material for preservation and information. This book lists Greenlandic mythological creatures alphabetically, A-U in accordance with the old Greenlandic alphabet. We decided early on to use only material gathered in Greenland. These stories come from sources all over Greenland and have been told to and by Greenlanders and outsiders, but the stories always originate from Greenland. By doing this, we could be sure that the creatures we have found really are Greenlandic—even if several of them are likely to have travelled with our ancestors from Canada and some even with the Norsemen and in time have become meshed in our own stories. There are many sources and many words for the same creature depending on where in the country the story stems from, many different descriptions of the creatures, as well as differences in old and more recent spellings. We have had to omit some details

The star of paganism has lost its shine, but it won't be extinguished as long as the northern lights dance in the sky, as long as storms rage and the swell beats the bedrock, as long as the wind, the current, and the torch of the sun send the icebergs drifting.

Jens Rosing

and included only features that the majority of sources agree on. As a result, this book isn't exhaustive, but it is a thorough and well-researched guide that can be used for both pleasure and education.

You can read the book from beginning to end, but you can also use it as a reference book for information on a particular creature. If you know of any creature, that is not included, please get in touch. I would love to learn more! At the back of the book, you will find a bibliography of the works in which they are mentioned, should you wish to explore further or just fancy reading the myths in which the creatures appear. When describing the creatures, we have used Greenlandic words and terms. These are marked in italics, and you will find an explanation of them in the Glossary. At the end of the book, you can also read more about the creative team behind this guide.

Many of the creatures are depicted in a style that challenges the way they have traditionally been interpreted. They may be ugly, scary, and even shocking—but then again that is the nature of creatures and spirits. We hope that you will enjoy the illustrations and have an experience beyond the ordinary. This guide seeks to gather and preserve traditional knowledge while at the same time challenging and renewing it.

I hope that the stories will stir your curiosity, provide you with new experiences, bring you joy, and last but not least, inspire you to use our huge collection of mythological creatures, spirits, and animals in novel and exciting ways.

Who knows what may be found in the heart of the deepest fjords where the world of mythology is still alive and thriving?

Maria Bach Kreutzmann

A BRIEF HISTORY OF GREENLAND

In the beginning it was ... cold

Greenland's history and landscape are shaped by paradoxical conditions: from several months of total darkness to some of constant light; from double-digit freezing temperatures to warm summers—well, relatively warm. Given how much vitamin D we need to even survive, the fact that people still live in Greenland today may surprise those who inhabit warmer and sunnier latitudes. Survival in Greenland has always required immense willpower, stamina, and determination, and there have been enormous losses along the way.

It could be argued that the early Greenlandic history, which begins about 2500 BCE, is characterized by a shocking amount of death. It is believed that six different cultures tried, unsuccessfully, to establish themselves in Greenland before the ancestors of today's Greenlanders made their arrival.

These cultures included the rather primitive Saqqaq, one of the first immigrant cultures. The Dorset and Late Dorset were exciting and fast-evolving cultures that may have met and inspired our Greenlandic ancestors in terms of spirit worshipping and artistic expression. One of the last immigrant cultures were the Norsemen—descendants of Icelandic Vikings—who would encounter our Greenlandic ancestors from time to time, and who very likely also inspired some hair-raising accounts of pale beings who lived to the far south of the land.

All these cultures had one thing in common: they failed to survive in Greenland's tough and often rapidly changing landscape. Their failure, however, is by no means surprising as the climate even today—despite every modern invention and precaution—can still cause whole towns to be abandoned for short or occasionally long periods.

This makes it all the more impressive that one culture managed not only to populate the country through slow, nomadic migration but also become the ancestor of today's Greenlanders: the Thule culture.

Tough culture—brutal nature

The Thule culture was in many respects a far superior culture compared to the previously mentioned early immigrants.

Most importantly, its people were extremely well adapted to the climate and the tough living conditions that resulted from it because they descended from people who, for hundreds of generations, had lived a nomadic life in the area around the Bering Strait between what is today Russia and Alaska.

The family structure was simple but strictly defined: men hunted, and women turned what the men caught into food, clothing, and anything else that was needed. Nothing from the hunt was wasted. Children were brought up according to these rules.

Summer, spring, and as much of the autumn as the weather permitted were spent travelling up and down the coast by *qajaq* and *umiaq* to hunt and gather food for the winter. A couple of families might travel and camp together, but it was also possible to camp slightly farther away from your family, an arrangement popular with young lovers. The custom of leaving your settlement during warmer weather also allowed people to meet at larger summer camps—known as *aasiviks*—in order to trade, build relationships, and exchange stories and experiences. There was also plenty of opportunity to exchange DNA—either through wife swapping or during *qaminngaarneq*, which means "the lights-out game." Both were customs designed to ensure strong and healthy offspring and to prevent inbreeding in a small and scattered population.

While the sun made various social get-togethers and different social structures possible, winter was restrictive. It was a time when one or two families might share a primitive cabin, and together they would see out the dark and cold months.

Winters could be brutal and commonly resulted in several deaths every year. Yet there was one thing that made the Thule culture far better equipped to life in the Arctic region than the previous settlers: they had perfected transport, which meant not only could they move faster and better than any previous culture, but they could also hunt much more efficiently. The *qajaq, the umiaq,* and the sledge, which enabled hunters to hunt and fish quickly and easily all year round, are well-known examples.

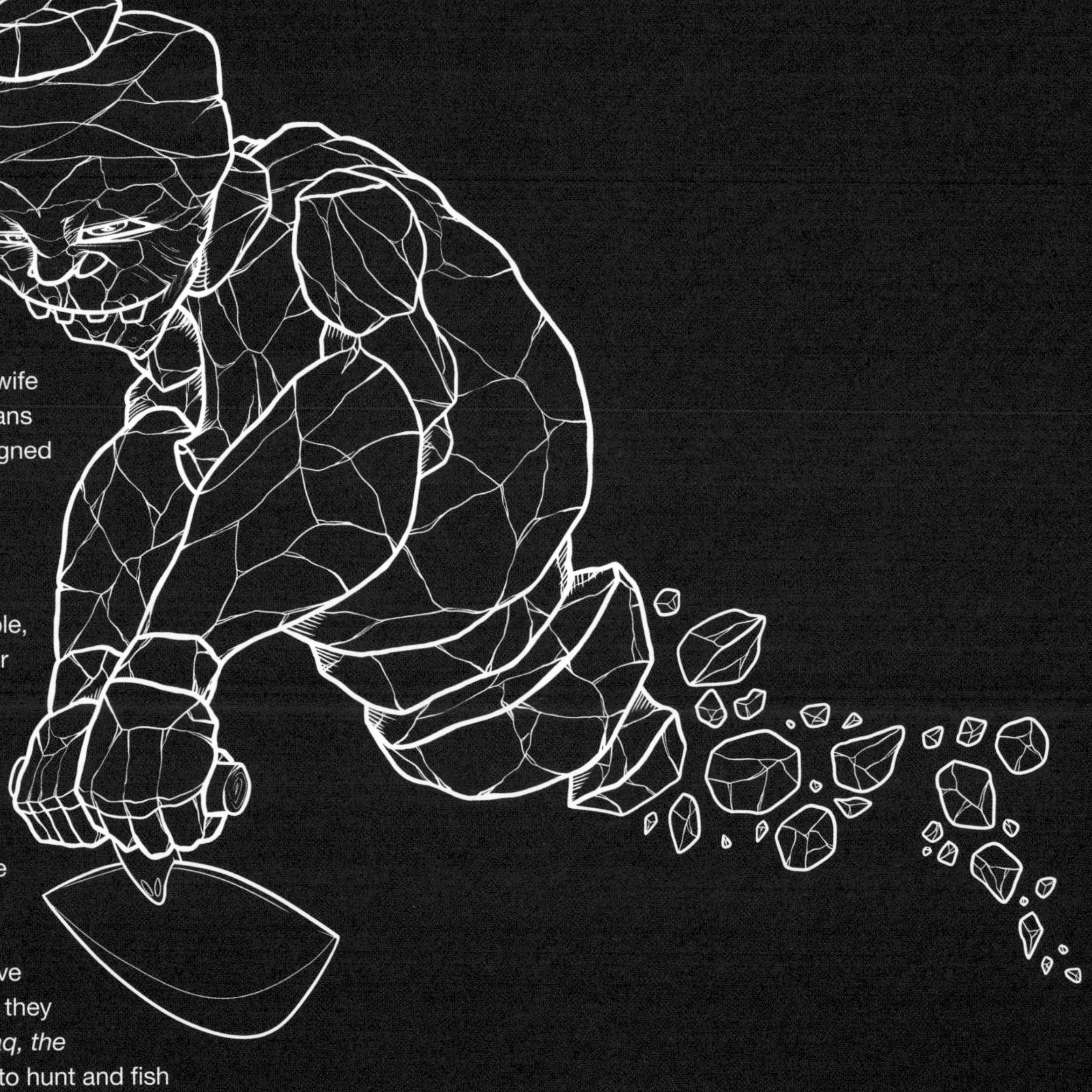

This improvement in hunting efficiency led to a more stable life, a life no longer dominated by the day-to-day survival that had characterized previous cultures. This in turn meant more time for other activities and new inventions in hunting, handicrafts, lifestyle, and especially entertainment.

As hunting methods improved, various forms of entertainment became a major and well-integrated part of the Thule culture because people now had the luxury of time–time to sing, to play, and to tell stories.

And yet the balance between exuberant survival and catastrophe and death remained a very delicate one …

Although the Thule culture was successful, surviving was hard work and lives were always at stake. The slightest change could have huge consequences, and nature continued to be one of the biggest threats: tough, capricious, and unforgiving, yet also beautiful and magnificent.

The Thule people were a hunter-gatherer culture with the emphasis on hunter. They depended completely on the animals they hunted and fished, which meant that even seemingly minor changes in the distribution of animals could mean feast or famine.

It is also important to bear in mind that the Thule culture wasn't a large population that arrived as one and then spread across Greenland but a collection of small groups consisting of a few families at most who lived together. As a result, these small communities were very vulnerable to change and to poor hunting and fishing.

Given that nature played such a huge role and was such a decisive force in their lives, it is no wonder that the Thule culture had to personify it and make it alive and tangible in an abundance of stories and myths.

Sila, spells, and taboos

A landscape that to some might seem a dead and a barren icey wasteland was to the Thule people teeming with creatures and spirits. Every single one of them had a special part to play or relationship to one another another as well as to the people, and with them came a confusion of taboos that had to be respected to avoid creating an imbalance.

At this point it should be stressed that the Thule people's view of the world can't be compared to an organized religion such as Christianity, for example, where one or several people can decide the truth and which rules must be followed. In order to explain the Thule culture's world view, the term *sila* is often used today. In Greenlandic, "*sila*" is a broad term that means weather, mind, world, and world order—but again, it would be wrong to regard *sila* as an actual religion.

For the Thule people, it was up to the individual family—in some cases, the individual person—to decide how to interpret the world, what the truth was, how to live, and what to submit to in order to maintain or restore the cosmic balance between the world of people and that of spirits.

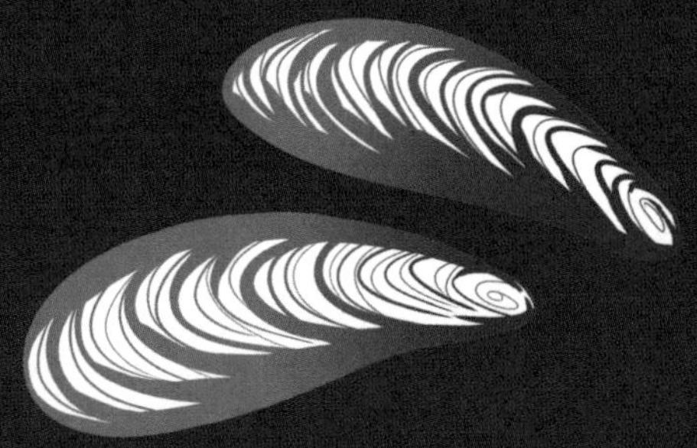

To this end, people had a number of strategies:

Taboos existed both for ordinary and special occasions. The rules relating to taboos were often complicated and difficult to carry out. Most were associated with daily tasks such as hunting and sewing, but they were followed most strictly on occasions such as birth and death. Unless they were observed, an imbalance that would trail much misfortune in its wake would be created.

Spells can be compared to a kind of prayer. They were not reserved for witches and *angakkut* but could be cast by anyone who had learned them. They were used to ward off accidents or summon help during difficult situations, but they could also be used to put curses on other people.

Amulets and tattoos, were used to either repel or attract the spirits, depending on how they were made and why. Evil spirits could be repelled by one kind of talisman, and good spirits could be attracted by another. Overall, women tended to favour tattoos, while men preferred amulets. This might be because women were regarded as being more closely connected to life or more vulnerable to the spirits due to their menstrual cycle and ability to create life.

Myths and stories could help you understand taboos and teach you how to use amulets and spells. The creatures, spirits, and animals they featured showed you how and why you must respect taboos, and they also served as a warning against certain types of behaviour. The stories and myths might change character and vary widely from place to place in order to make them most relevant to the situation in which they were told or the composition of their audience. Thus they were not simply good entertainment during long, dark winter nights but also the *truth*—and you had better take them seriously.

If the creatures and the stories in this guide don't match your understanding, it might be due to differences in the oral narrative passed down for generations and in the retellings of the retellings that were first written down by different missionaries, catechists, and explorers during the eighteenth and twentieth centuries. The Europeans who wrote them down invariably had their own understanding and interpretation of the myths they were told—something which has undoubtedly influenced their accounts—not to mention a level of censorship many found it necessary to introduce when the stories became too salacious. Furthermore, every story would be told with local colour and in the storyteller's personal style.

Written sources totalling more than 15,000 pages form the basis for this book. The material has been carefully chosen and reviewed based on criteria such as geography and critical comparisons of as many sources as possible. We have included as much information as we could on each creature—some are mentioned by only a single source, others by several. Some creatures have contradictory descriptions and characteristics. This might be due to geography, the collector's own interpretation, or some other reason, but everything has been considered in this guide. Although the Greenlandic world of myths and spirits has much in common with other Inuit, we have focused exclusively on Greenlandic stories.

Ujammiugaq Engell

MYTHICAL CREATURES, SPIRITS, AND ANIMALS **A-U**

AAJUMAAQ

[²a: ju ²mɑ:q#] The sleeved one

AAJUMAAQ is known and feared across all of Greenland; it has served as a helper spirit to some of the greatest *angakkut* such as *Naaja, Maratsi, Missuarniannga, Akku,* and others. Its body is similar to that of a human being, but it has long, slender arms that are black from the elbows down. Each hand has only three fingers and each foot only three toes. The head is described as a bald dog's head or as a skeletal dog's head with large, piercing eyes. It floats across the ground, and everything touched by its long fingers soon rots, including people. It speaks like a whispering ghost but can also be very loud when it announces its arrival, shouting: "*Attungara Aajumaartoq!* Anything I touch will rot!" When not helping an *angakkoq* with his work, it likes to live in a tunnel in the ice cap.

There are many different stories where *AAJUMAAQ* not only acts as a helper spirit but also as a creature of vengeance when an *angakkoq* uses it to attack his enemies. It often accompanies an *angakkoq* on their spirit journey to the other world as its strength makes it a powerful weapon against evil spirits or enemies wanting to kill the *angakkoq* on his travels. But first the *angakkoq* needs to master or ally with the helper spirit.

MISSUARNIANNGA WENT INTO THE MOUNTAINS looking for *AAJUMAAQ*, knowing full well that trying to master it could prove very dangerous. He sat down on a rock near a ravine and was seized by a dreadful terror. It made him shake uncontrollably, but he didn't know what exactly had induced such fear in him. Suddenly the ravine started to move, and he heard *AAJUMAAQ* scream a warning from the deep. The creature slowly emerged with its long, black arms reaching out for him. Petrified, *Missuarniannga* sat very still and let *AAJUMAAQ* get very close to him, but he fainted as the creature floated over him. When he came round, it had disappeared, but he returned to the ravine on two other occasions, and when he had seen and repeated its name three times, it became his helper spirit.

AASSIK

[²a:s sik#] The giant worm

AASSIK is a giant worm that appears in many different stories across Greenland. It is so big that the earth around it trembles when it is killed, and its meat is described as almost pure blubber. It has impressive stamina and can pull heavy loads without stopping, which makes it the perfect draft animal, although it can be very temperamental and as a result it requires great strength and patience to tame it. It is easily angered and can be very dangerous to strangers, so the driver of the worm must keep it far away from any passengers on his sledge. It is often found near the dogs' hitching posts, where it lives in a hole underground and tries to eat the puppies.

There are stories about *AASSIK* with and without human features, something it has in common with many other Greenlandic mythological figures.

A WOMAN WAS FORCED to marry an *AASSIK* with a human face. They had twins, and their children's children still had its characteristic mask. When you look at a butterfly caterpillar today, you can clearly see the outline of a human face.

A WOMAN WAS ABDUCTED, and her brother got an *AASSIK*, an *AMAROQ*, and a polar bear to pull his sledge so that it would go faster. The polar bear, the only non-supernatural creature of the three, tired first. For that reason, it was a great help in the old days to find a strong creature to pull your sledge.

AAVERPAK

[^{2}a: ^{1}vɜp pak#] The giant walrus

AAVERPAK is a giant walrus that often turns up in connection with a spirit journey or when an apprentice undergoes his last test to become a full-fledged *angakkoq*.

In East Greenland, it is better known as *AAFFAFFAQ*, and it is sometimes described as having short, stubby legs and a horn on its nose or on its back rather than the familiar long tusks of the walrus.

It is often found with *NAPPAASILAT*, and together they will help an *angakkoq* on his journey to the spirit world, either by eating him or throwing him around.

A YOUNG MAN was afraid to be eaten by *AAVERPAK* and *NAPPAASILAT* during his training and kept postponing his spirit journey. When he finally plucked up the courage, *NAPPAASILAT* appeared in his trance and dragged him down to the shore by his testicles. Here it threw him into the sea to *AAVERPAK*, who sank its tusks in under his collarbone. Meanwhile, *NAPPAASILAT* had reached the sea and caught the young man, who was thrown back and forth between them. Their game ended up with the young man being hurled to the edge of the sky. No wonder he dreaded his spirit journey.

AJAQQISAAQ

[a ¹jaq qi ²sɑ:q#]

AJAQQISAAQ is an inherited helper spirit. Not much is known about its appearance, but it often guides an *angakkoq* on his spirit journey.

AGGU, AN *ANGAKKOQ*, WENT on a guided journey to the Land of the Dead in the sky and the Land of the Dead in the sea to see the difference between dying on land and in water. There he met his father, from whom he inherited *AJAQQISAAQ*.

AKUEQQUTIT

[a ku ¹wɜq qu tsit#] Those you can't get rid of

AKUEQQUTIT are a kind of inverted conscience that make you do only bad things. They can appear in the shape of a man, a woman, and even a child. They are so thoroughly malicious that no flesh can grow on them.

These spirits walk at everybody's heels, and whenever you feel an urge to do something you know you are not allowed to do, they will whisper in your ear, "Go on, go on, do it!" It is very tempting to give in to them. Their only aim is to make sure that people do the wrong or forbidden things.

ALLAQ

[ˈaɬ ɬɑq#] The bear on land

An *ALLAQ* is a female *QIVITTOQ*. Unlike a man, a woman's appearance will change dramatically if she turns into a *QIVITTOQ*: one half of her remains human, while the other half becomes a polar bear. Whether this is vertically or horizontally differs from story to story. A woman becomes very wide and her mouths fill with blood and snot, which might be covered up with a *kamik*, and she will shriek loudly when she attacks. You may be able to keep an *ALLAQ* at bay by wearing the clothes of a dead person, which acts as a kind of amulet. *ALLAQ* can be hugely territorial and are fond of guarding places rich in black crowberries and blueberries.

When a woman wants to become a *QIVITTOQ*, she will go to the mountains, where she will die from the cold after five days. After that, she comes alive as an *ALLAQ* and will never feel the cold again.

AN *ALLAQ* WAS ATTACKED by another *QIVITTOQ* that landed a well-placed kick on her human half, sending her over a cliff edge. On the way down, she roared like a bear when her bear half hit the rocks and screamed like a woman when her human side got hurt.

See *INNERSUIT & ALLIARUTSIT*

AMAARSISARTOQ

[a ²mɑːs si ¹sɑt tɔq#] The hooded one

An *AMAARSISARTOQ* steals newborn babies and sometimes an *angakkoq* on a spirit journey by putting them into its huge *amaat*. *AMAARSISARTOQ* seem to be attracted by boiling food. To ward it off, you are advised to hang up a mussel shell if you are cooking in a house with a woman who has just given birth.

WHEN A FAMILY KEPT losing its newborn babies, they contacted an *angakkoq*. The *angakkoq's* job was to look for the children, and in *AMAARSISARTOQ'S* house. The *angakkoq* brought the children back but decided to return to the house, only to be snatched by the creature, which put the *angakkoq* in its hood. The *angakkoq* summoned all his helper spirits, but they were driven back one by one. The only one capable of attacking was the falcon, which pecked away mercilessly at *AMAARSISARTOQ'S* forehead. This enabled the *angakkoq* to escape and kill *AMAARSISARTOQ*.

AMAROQ

[a mɑ ʁɔq#] The wolf

AMAROQ is a giant wolf that haunts the edge of the ice cap and the ice cap itself. It likes to make its den on plains with cotton grass. Here it feeds on reindeer, and it is so big that it can carry a whole reindeer in its mouth. It can be a great threat to people when it hunts as it likes to have the reindeer all to itself. If an area suddenly loses its reindeer population, people will often wonder if an *AMAROQ* is about. If you hurt it or its offspring, it might take revenge by stealing your soul.

AMAROQS have been described as being able to change shape from human to wolf, or else convincingly disguise themselves as humans. When in human form or guise, they are described as skilled reindeer hunters. At times, people catch them to use them as draft animals along with an *AASSIK*. The Arctic wolf isn't native to West Greenland, only to East Greenland, and this might explain why the wolf is a mythological being in stories from the west coast.

In one story, the *AMAROQ* is a kind of spiritual port back to life. When a young man capsizes in his *qajaq* on a lake while out hunting reindeer, a pack of *AMAROQ* offspring eat his body, and their old *AMAROQ* grandmother gathers their excrement and covers it with moss. The man is brought back to life and is a skilled reindeer hunter from that day onward.

A YOUNG WOMAN disappeared from her settlement. Her father went to look for her and discovered that she was living in a beautiful house completely covered by reindeer fur. Her father crept up to the house and peeked through the window, where he saw his daughter sitting with her little son on even more reindeer furs. As she didn't seem to be in distress, he went home. Meanwhile, the young woman had started to wonder why her husband was so good at hunting reindeer, so she secretly followed him to see what he did. She was heading toward the ice cap when she spotted him on a great plain and saw him turn from a human being into a huge wolf. She was terrified at the sight and fled with her son back to her parents' settlement.

AMU

[a mu#]

AMU is like *AAJUMAAQ,* a helper spirit known across all of Greenland. It appears in many different stories and has a distinctive appearance: a small, almost withered body; two extremely long arms with three fingers on each hand; and a big head with large, shiny eyes. An *AMU*'s presence is easy to detect as it continually screams "*Amuuuu! Amuuuu!*"

An *angakkoq* might embark on a spirit journey to find a spirit causing bad luck at a settlement. In order to go on the journey, the *angakkoq*'s soul needs to leave the body, so the *angakkoq* performs a ritual with people from the settlement. During this ritual, the primary function of the *AMU* is to keep the audience alive and protect them from external spirits or any spirits that might be hiding in the room.

As with *AAJUMAAQ*, an *angakkoq* must defeat an *AMU* to turn it into a helper spirit.

ANGIUT

[¹a ŋi jut#]

ANGIUT is a helper spirit who speaks like a human being. It resembles a small seal but has a skeletal head.

It can help an *angakkoq* by identifying a disease, discovering who is ailing from which disease, or finding out if anyone is in distress and needs help.

MISSUARNIANNGA WAS BUSY gathering helper spirits and decided to get an *ANGIUT*. He went to the mountains and started rubbing a black-and-white stone against a rock. He did that for a long time, and at last it felt as though the rock he was rubbing grew soft while at the same time it started to disappear into the mountain. He picked up the stone and discovered that a hole had opened up in the mountain. Suddenly an *ANGIUT* popped its head out of the hole. It chatted to him for a while, then *Missuarniannga* put the stone back in the hole and went home. He came back the next day, and when he had summoned the *ANGIUT* for the third time, it became his helper spirit.

ANINGAAQ

[ɛ ni ²ŋɑ:q#] The man on the moon

ANINGAAQ is one of the best-known mythical figures in Greenland and appears in a wealth of stories playing different parts. He is often described as either being dressed in an *ikiaq* or several layers of bear skin. Seals with white spots may be hunted only by him, and he has been known to kill anyone ignoring this rule.
He happens to be scared of catfish.

Just like *SASSUMA ARNAA,* he guards the animals that people hunt and fish, and makes sure that people respect his taboos.
If someone breaks a taboo, he has been known to send his huge dog after that person or a whole settlement as a form of collective punishment. If he sets out to inflict punishments himself, he carries a big, black wooden stick, which he uses to tear down house walls.
To defend yourself against him, you must try and wrench the stick from him. If you know that he is on his way, you must extinguish all lamps immediately so he can't see where you are. He also helps with infertility and has been known to impregnate women who struggle to have children or are unmarried.

His house is on the moon, and you can reach it either on a spirit journey or by getting your directions directly from *ANINGAAQ.*
But you must be very careful not to get lost going up there as you risk being eaten by the dreaded *ERLAVEERSINIOOQ.*

ANINGAAQ was turned into the man on the moon because he had an incestuous relationship with his sister *MALIINA*, who became the sun.

A YOUNG WOMAN was ordered onto *ANINGAAQ*'s sledge and abducted to his house on the moon. When they arrived, he put her on a big reindeer fur and lay on top of her so she passed out. When she came round, he showed her a hatch in the floor through which she could see all life on earth. He told her that he would send her back to earth, where she would give birth to a baby boy. When the boy was old enough, *ANINGAAQ* would come for him and take him back to the moon, so the boy could look after him in his old age.

ANNGIAQ

[ˈaŋ ŋi jɑq#] The secret

An *ANNGIAQ* is a scare spirit. It is a baby or fetus born in secret and then killed. Its spirit lives on, looking for the love of which it was robbed. It finds a dog skull, which it uses as its *qajaq*. It chases its relatives when they are out sailing in order to pull them under the water and drown them or shoot them with a bow and arrow as a punishment for their misdeed. It can also crawl into any siblings born after it and kill them by causing internal bleeding.

An *ANNGIAQ* can only be vanquished if the woman who gave birth in secret admits what she has done and thus reveals the secret. The defeated *ANNGIAQ* is then said to be useful as an amulet to increase, say, the speed of your *qajaq*.

A YOUNG WOMAN whose father was a great *angakkoq* remained unmarried because her father couldn't find any man worthy of her. She fell secretly in love with a young man and became pregnant without her father knowing. She was troubled by strong stomach pains and told her parents that she had to go outside to do her business undisturbed. She gave birth to a baby boy whom she killed and buried. When she later found a man and was married, all the children she gave birth to died. In order to hide what she had done, she accused her sister-in-law of having created an *ANNGIAQ*, but when another *angakkoq* went on a spirit journey and saw what had really happened, she was finally forced to confess.

AQAJARORMIORSIORTOQ

[ɑ qa jɑ ¹ʁɔm mi ¹jɔs si ¹jɔt tɔq#] The stone troll

AQAJARORMIORSIORTOQ is a troll whose entire body is made from stone except the corner of its mouth. This is where you need to hit it to kill it. It lives in a cave in the ice cap and carries a big *ulu*, which it bashes against things, making a loud, echoing noise.

When it appears, it can frighten a whole settlement to death if they so much as look at it.

ARPATTUT

[¹ɑp ¹pat tut#] The runners

An *ARPATTUT* attack is often immediately preceded by reflections or mirages that appear on the surface of the water. They arrive in big *umiat* and carry shiny weapons, which they use to eradicate whole settlements.

TWO ORPHANS HAD GONE to fetch water when the younger child suddenly saw faces reflected in the water. The older child didn't believe her at first, but soon he, too, saw the reflections and could feel from the movement of the water that someone was coming. They fled back to the settlement and told everyone what had happened, but no one believed them. The two orphans hid in the wood shavings in the common house and were the only two to survive.

ASIAQ

[1a si jaq#] The wind

ASIAQ rules the wind and the weather. Her mouth sits vertically on her face and her eyes and nose across it horizontally. Even her hair is the wrong way, and she has a hollow back. Everything about her is generally topsy-turvy, even in her house: her bed is upside down and her blubber lamp points downward.

She is said to be a woman who has wandered the earth since the dawn of time looking for a husband, but her search is always in vain as nobody wants someone with a crooked face. As a result, she stole a child from another woman and brought him up in order to marry him. Her husband is enormous and wears many bracelets, but *ASIAQ* can turn him into a baby again whenever she feels threatened. She gets food by stealing it from people's underground meat stores using a magic glove and a magic bag.

A SETTLEMENT WAS PLAGUED by bad weather and too much snow. *Naaja*, an *angakkoq*, decided to go on a spirit journey with his spirit helpers to *ASIAQ*'s house to ask for her help. *ASIAQ* agreed to help and took a piece of bear skin on which her child-husband had urinated and shook it forcefully while she whispered rain sounds, after which it started to rain on the earth and the snow melted. However, the *angakkoq* was forced to stop her eventually as the rain would otherwise have lasted several months—or it would never have stopped raining at all.

ASSAGISSAT

[¹as sa ¹ɣis sat#] The crayfish animal

ASSAGISSAT is a helper spirit that looks like a crayfish or has claw hands. It is used for hunting *TUPILAAT*.

EQALUSSUAQ

[ɜ qa ˈlus su wɑq#] The shark fish

EQALUSSUAQ is a fish spirit shaped like a Greenlandic shark. It protects orphans, single women, and widows, and it makes sure to feed them when they are starving.

It can crawl over land and dive and swim in inland lakes when it needs to, and it has been known to take a human wife.

TWO ORPHANS WERE LEFT BEHIND at a settlement when none of the other families were able to provide for them. They survived by eating black crowberries and a little ammassat, which their former foster mother had given them, but soon winter came and they began to starve. One night while a snowstorm was raging, they heard a noise in the passage, and a big EQALUSSUAQ turned up with a piece of meat in its mouth. EQALUSSUAQ fed them and told them to come with it to its house, where it had enough food for them to survive the winter. One day the EQALUSSUAQ didn't come home.It had been hunted and eaten by a sperm whale, but the children were found and adopted by a new family.

EQQILLIT

[^{1}ɜq ^{1}qiɬ ɬit#] The dog people

EQQILLIT are half-dog, half-human creatures found in big packs on the ice cap. Sometimes they live in ordinary houses; at other times they prefer caves under big rocks near the ice cap or on the ice cap itself. They can move at great speed and easily outrun a human trying to escape them. Their sense of smell is just like a dog's, so be careful when you are out on the ice cap, especially if you are a menstruating woman as they are known to attack and rape. If you want to sneak up on an *EQQILIK*, make sure to do so when it is busy having sex and oblivious to its surroundings. Otherwise it is very hard to ambush.

They can be extremely aggressive and hostile and love to pick fights with people from the coast. They are experts at using weapons, especially bows, but they are also skilled in making knives and *ulut*, a trading item much in demand. They will often steal food and equipment. However, they fear sled dogs, which can be used to ward them off. They are particularly fond of seal brains.

A WOMAN REFUSED to get married, and her father suspected her of having sex with her dog. He spied on her and soon discovered that his suspicion was well founded. In all secrecy she gave birth to a litter of ten, whom her father grew to love because they could help him pull his *qajaq* out of the water when he came home with his catch. Yet the woman was bitter and resentful, and she convinced the children to kill and eat her father one day when he came home from a long hunting trip. She cast a spell on a *kamik* sole and sent half her children out to sea. The *kamik* sole turned into a boat that drifted to foreign shores. Here the puppies turned into *qallunaat*, and all *qallunaat* are said to be their descendants. She sent the rest to the ice cap, where they became the ancestors of all *EQQILLIT*.

EQUNGASOQ

[ɜ ^{1}qu ŋa sɔq#]
The one with the crooked mouth

EQUNGASOQ is a very clever helper spirit that can tell an *angakkoq* of things to come and lead the *angakkoq* to the Land of the Dead. It has a big, crooked mouth placed vertically across its face, and it gets very upset if you ask any questions about it.

It lives on the farthest rocks from the sea, which it will leave only when the waves are very high. It is a useful spirit to summon should you get into difficulties during a storm. When you call it, it turns up in a shower of sparks.

ERLAVEERSINIOOQ

[^{1}ɜɬ ɬa ^{2}vɜːs si ni ^{2}jɔːq#] The gut eater

ERLAVEERSINIOOQ is sometimes described as a hideous and grotesque old crone; at other times she is merely a woman with a face that is wider than it is long or longer than it is wide. When she turns around, you can see her huge crotch and when she bends forwards, she licks her own bottom. When she bends to the side, her cheek will slap loudly against her hip. One or two big sculpins hang from her groin and they swing from side to side when she walks. She will attack anyone who laughs, and will try and make a person laugh when she beats a *qilaat* with her *ulu*. If there is even a hint of a smile at the corner of a person's mouth, she will cut out their intestines, liver, or other organs through one large gash across the belly.

Her house lies west of the moon, and if you get lost on your way to *ANINGAAQ*, you risk being caught by *ERLAVEERSINIOOQ*. She has a big dish in which she puts the intestines when she has cut them out, and that dish comes jumping into the room when she summons it.

A MARRIED COUPLE BROKE *ANINGAAQ*'s taboo, knowing full well that he would come after them. When *ANINGAAQ* reached the couple's house, the husband managed to defeat him in a wrestling match and was then invited to visit his house on the moon. *ANINGAAQ* stressed how important it was that the husband go the right way past the moon, but still the husband got lost and ran into *ERLAVEERSINIOOQ*. He tried hard not to laugh when she danced in front of him, but he couldn't help smiling at her bizarre movements. At that moment she pounced and ripped out his lungs. She put the lungs aside to cool down, but the man managed to snatch them back and escape, and he survived by eating his own lungs.

IGALILIK

[i ¹ɣa li lik#] The pot creature

IGALILIK carries a big pot of hot rocks on its shoulders for cooking. *IGALILIK* can carry the pot even when it is boiling as the heat doesn't seem to bother the creature at all. It lives inland, where it likes to pick up seagull chicks from the ground and boil them in its pot. On warm days it will also wander around and catch salmon in the rivers.

IGALILIK is rarely a friendly creature. In self-defence it will collapse in on itself so that only its chin and knees can be seen.

IKKIILLINEQANNGEQQISSAARTOQ

[¹ik ²kiːɬ ɬi nɜ ¹qaŋ ¹ŋɜq ¹qis ²sɑːt tɔq#] The one that never gets blunt

IKKIILLINEQANNGEQQISSAARTOQ is a creature with an incredibly sharp saw or a long, pointy knife blade on its back. To defend itself, it will jump up with its back to its attacker and cut them.

It lives between big rocks, inside rocky caves, or in the deep crevasses of the ice cap.

A YOUNG MAN'S SISTER was abducted by a giant. To bring her back, her brother fetched three creatures to pull his sledge: a polar bear, a *PARPALIGAMIK UNIAKATTALIK*, and an *IKKIILLINEQANNGEQQISSAARTOQ*. He found the giant and made the creatures attack him. *IKKIILLINEQANNGEQQISSAARTOQ* sawed open the giant's stomach, and thus the young man rescued his sister.

IKUSIK

[i ku sik#] The one that crawls on its elbows

An *IKUSIK* is a corpse that crawls along on its elbows because its forearms have rotted away. It drags its feet behind it, but it can still move at great speed if it needs to and catch a grown person running. It hunts humans and eats them alive, usually because they have desecrated its grave.

ILLUKOQ

[ˈiɬ ɬu kɔq#] The half one

ILLUKOQ is a half human, split vertically. Despite its missing half, it is very agile, leaping easily from ice floe to ice floe, and in a *qajaq* it can paddle as fast as a whole human being.

It likes to visit people and entertain them by telling stories. It expects to be offered generous hospitality, but it loathes half-rotten boiled cod.

IMMAP NANUA

[¹im map# na nu wa#] The bear of the sea

IMMAP NANUA is a huge polar bear. It is not to be confused with *NAPPAASILAT* or *SERMILISSUAQ* because this bear is so big that it can wade through fjords and only get wet up to its waist. If it puts its front paws on the shore and cranes its neck, it can lick the highest mountaintops.

If it sticks its head out of the sea just as an *umiaq* is passing, it can suck the *umiaq* and any surrounding icebergs into its enormous nostrils when it breathes in or tip out all paddlers when it breathes out. If it sees any people, regardless of whether they are out on the water or walking ashore, it will come after them and though it is enormous, it is completely silent, so most of the time you won't notice it until it is too late.

AN ORPHAN BOY WAS out picking berries with the other children from his settlement when he suddenly spotted *IMMAP NANUA* heading toward them. The orphan boy herded all the other children into a big crevice in the mountain and placed himself at the top as he didn't think anyone would miss him if he was eaten. The bear swallowed the orphan boy and lumbered back to the water, never noticing the other children. They climbed out of the crevice, ran home to their settlement, and told everyone what the orphan boy had done. The orphan boy was now sitting inside the belly of the bear, which was so big that he could stand up and walk about. His hair began to fall off as the belly of the bear was so hot that it almost burned him. He wandered around for a while until he remembered that he had a small knife in his pocket. He started to cut a hole in the belly of the bear in order to get out. The bear's belly filled with blood, and just as the boy thought he would drown, he finally managed to make the hole big enough to escape. The very same second he set foot on the ground, the enormous bear dropped down dead. Meanwhile, the people from the settlement had started mourning the boy and gone to look for his body. When they found him alive and the bear dead, they were delighted. *IMMAP NANUA* was so big that its skin could line several *qaannat* and *umiat* and pay for a whole team of dogs. From then on the orphan boy was known as a great hunter.

INNERSUIT & ALLIARUTSIT

[^{1}in ^{1}nɜs su wit# & ^{1}aɬ ɬi jɑ ^{1}ʁut tsit#] The fire people

INNERSUIT are small spirits that live just below the seashore or out on the rocks in beautiful and tidy houses. They have small noses, hollow cheeks, very pale or blue eyes, and human forms. On a night when the moon is bright, you can see *INNERSUIT* from far away as their veins glow like fire. When you hear the squealing sound of the ice grating against the rocks by the shore, it is really the *INNERSUIT* that are crying. If they feel threatened, they can make themselves invisible, unless they want to be helper spirits to an *angakkoq*.

In addition to acting as helper spirits, *INNERSUIT* themselves have spiritual powers and can have their own helper spirits. They are very friendly and happy to help people whenever they can; they may even trade with them.

ALLIARUTSIT are closely related to *INNERSUIT* but are more formidable creatures. They live at the bottom of the sea near the shore. They are big and look like humans, but they have no noses or hair. They can also make themselves invisible. They are exceptional *qajaq* rowers and are capable of paddling under the sea and up again. They are often used as helper spirits by an *angakkoq* as their spiritual abilities enable them to both defend the *angakkoq* and avenge him. When not acting as helper spirits, they might abduct a *qajaq* rower and keep him captive.

They have been known to cut the noses off the people they abduct out of jealousy. If a man suddenly feels a strong current during a *qajaq* trip, it is the *ALLIARUTSIT* trying to abduct him. If he doesn't get free of the current and is pulled under, he must refrain from eating or drinking for five days or he can never return to the Land of the Living again.

Some people believe that *ALLIARUTSIT* and *INNERSUIT* are the same creatures and that the different names are merely the result of variations in dialects. But in several places they are considered separate as people will often talk of *ALLIARUTSIT* as "the *INNERSUIT* below," which is taken to mean that they live below the *INNERSUIT* by the shore. Besides, the *ALLIARUTSIT* are often described as more formidable than the *INNERSUIT*.

INNERSUIT TAARTAAT

[¹in ¹nɜs su wit# ²tɑ:t ²ta:t#]

Helper spirits to the fire people

Just like *angakkut*, *INNERSUIT* have their own helper spirits. They are known as *INNERSUIT TAARTAAT*. They have wide mouths and wear white anoraks with red neck lining. They are skilled rowers and will often attack *qajaq* rowers, but they can be chased away using an *EQUNGASOQ*.

INORROOQ

[i ^{1}nɔχ ^{2}χɔ:q#] The shape shifter

INORROOQ is an animal that can change its shape so that it resembles a human being. When in its human form, it is reminiscent of the animal it was before it changed.

Hares, ravens, and ptarmigan can all be *INORROOQ* and will often change to help people in distress.

A YOUNG WOMAN was going to marry a captain but overslept on the day she was due to meet his ship. When she got to the sea, she saw that the ship had sailed without her, and she grew very sad. She met a young woman with very dark skin wearing black clothing and blue-and-black *kamiit*. This woman carried a child in an *amaat*, had a child in her arms, and had another child walking by her side. She invited the sad woman to her home for dinner. They reached a beautiful, small house, and the woman in the dark clothing started to tidy and tell stories to cheer up the sad woman. Suddenly they heard a loud crash. The sad woman rushed outside and saw that the mountain on which the house was built was now completely enveloped in fog. She turned around only to find that the house was gone. All that was left was a mound of earth with ravens flying off.

INORUTSIT

[i nɔ ¹ʁut tsit#] The inland giants

INORUTSIT are giants that live inland and wear only clothes made of sealskin with the hairs removed. They look very much like people, but in some stories they each have only one eye.

Their language is somewhat different from human language, which can cause considerable misunderstanding and confusion. They are rarely friendly and have been known to kidnap and eat people.

A YOUNG WOMAN was abducted by an *INORUSEQ* when she was out fishing salmon in the river. He carried her home to his house and put her on a couch where she was told to stay until she stopped crying. An old *INORUSEQ* woman appeared from behind a curtain and offered her reindeer tallow and fox and hare testicles to eat, but the young woman refused. The old woman scolded her and was trying to stop her crying when an *INUSSUAQ SAARNGIINNAQ* came crawling out from behind the curtain and warned her to do as she was told or she would end up like him. The old woman held up a pair of *kamiit* full of worms, spiders, and water beetles and threatened to make the young woman wear them so that the insects could eat all the flesh on her legs. The young woman got furious and stamped on the boots until they broke. The *INORUSEQ* who had abducted the woman then married her. Her new family watched her carefully, but after some time she gained the freedom to wander about. Finally, she managed to escape and find her way back to her own family.

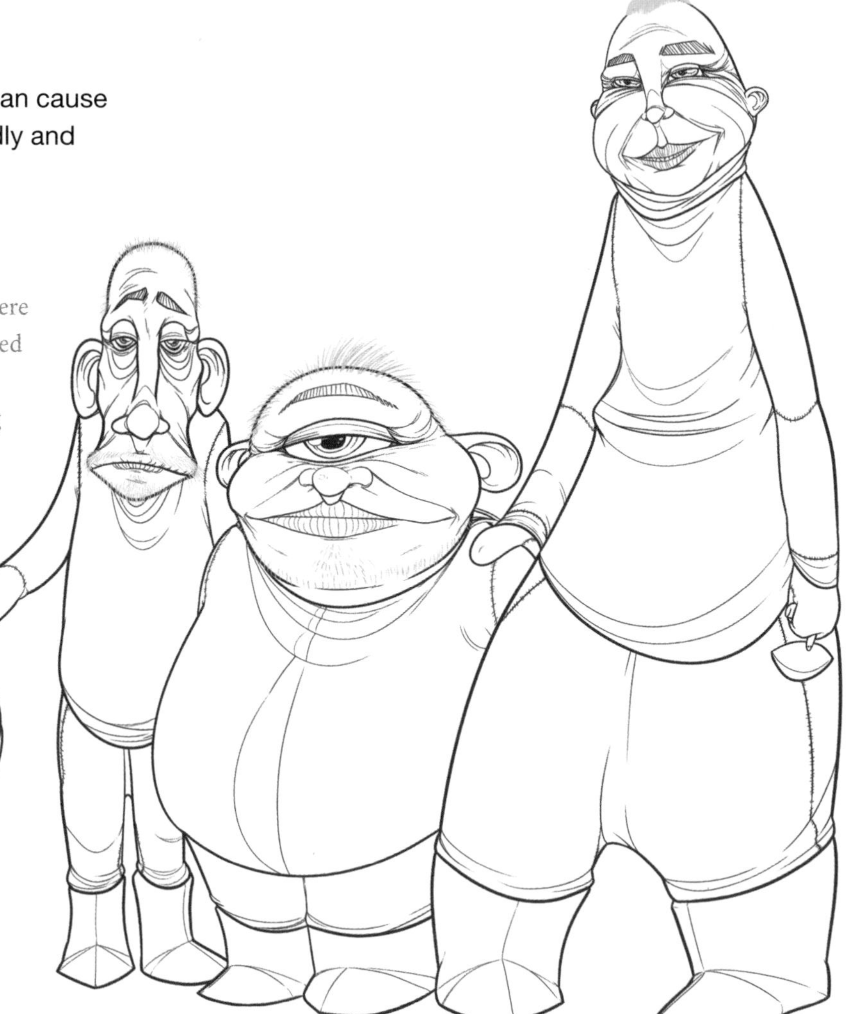

INUARAKASIK

[i nu wɑ ˈʁa ka sik#]
The little one that can do anything

INUARAKASIK is a small, human-like helper spirit to the great *angakkoq Aattaaritaa*.

AATTAARITAA DECIDED TO travel to the west coast to be converted to Christianity—much to the irritation of his helper spirits. If he became a Christian, he would no longer be able to see them or receive their help. One day when he was preparing for his journey, he felt something touch his legs. He looked down and saw an *INUARAKASIK* that asked him why he was going. *Aattaaritaa* said that he had had a vision of the end of the world and that he had to let himself be baptized as he feared burning in hell. "If the world ends, I promise to start it again!" the *INUARAKASIK* promised him. But *Aattaaritaa* decided to be baptized after all and thus turned his back on the spirit world.

INUARULLIKKAT

[i nu wɑ ¹ʁuɬ ¹ɬik kat#] The small, clumsy ones

INUARULLIKKAT are small and very clumsy creatures who wear bright and colourful clothes, often in shades of blue. They also have another outfit that is more practical: whenever they have to carry something heavy, they put on big anoraks and become just as big as humans. When they have finished their work, they take off their anoraks and return to their original size. They each carry a hollow stick, which they use as a kind of weapon by pointing with it. At one end of the stick, there is a small, black stone with a red stone on top. This weapon is so dangerous that they always hold it in their left hand so they do not risk hurting others accidentally. If they point the stick at a human being in anger, that person will drop dead straight away.

In spring and summer they wander far and wide, and if they need to sail, they do so in a boat made from stone. In the winter they live in small caves in the ground, but they can make their caves bigger by rubbing them should they get a visit from anyone taller than themselves. Every now and then they act as helper spirits to an *angakkoq* and might even make barren women pregnant by crawling inside them.

When they get old, they throw themselves down a mountainside and regain their youth. They can do this five times in total, after which they really die of old age.

INUSSUAQ SAARNGIINNAQ

[i ¹nus su waq# ²sa:ŋ ¹ŋin naq#] The bone man

INUSSUAQ SAARNGIINNAQ is a skeletal creature that will sometimes approach men out hunting. It is so terrifying that you can die from fear when you talk about having seen it.

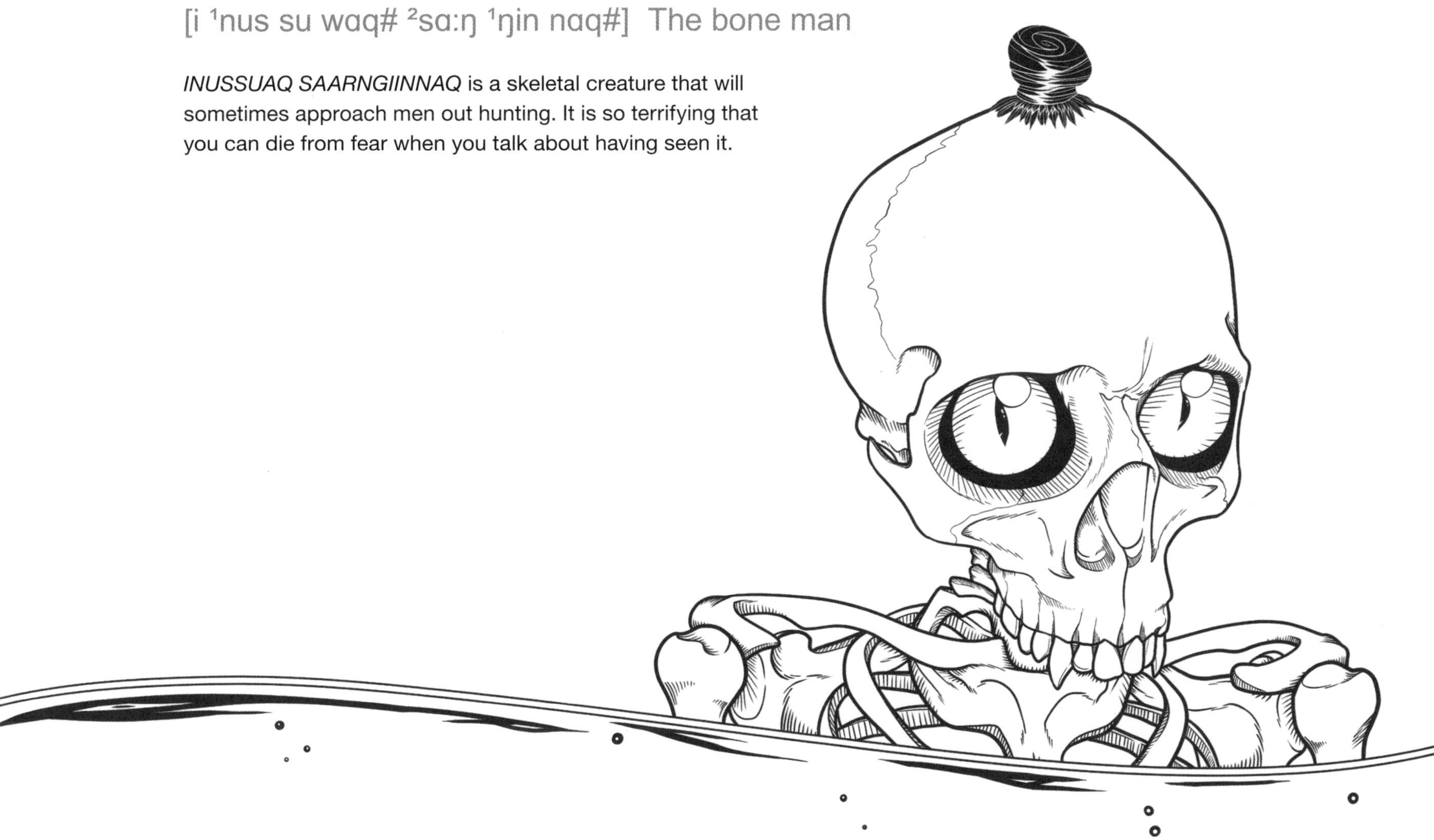

ISEQQAT

[i ¹s3q qat#] The little tumblers

ISEQQAT are tiny creatures no taller than the length of a man's forearm. They are shiny and have dark faces. They usually run around naked. Their eyes are sideways on their faces so they wink vertically, and they have no noses. Their bodies are soft, and they each have only one orifice, which they use for urinating. This applies to *ISEQQAT* of both sexes.

They love teasing and hiding out in people's pantries, where they steal food such as dried fish and seal blood. When not hiding among humans, they live in rocky crevices or underground. If they feel threatened, they inflate themselves until they become as big as people, but they can also get stressed and die of fright if they are captured.

AN OLD WOMAN TOLD A STORY about the time she was woken up by *ISEQQAT*. It happened when she was a little girl, and the *ISEQQAT* had tickled her feet while she was asleep. When she woke up, she chased after them to catch them, but they managed to disappear into a crack in the wall.

ITTUKU

[¹it tu ku#] The iron giant

ITTUKU is a one-legged giant who lives on an island with his wife. He is dressed in iron and always carries beautiful tools. He can talk to the migrating birds that fly past his house, but he also has a taste for boiled bird meat.

When ships pass his house, he shouts at them. If they shout back, he will let them pass, but if they ignore him, he will regard them as his enemies and lasso them with his enormous whip to reel them in. He will then force them to unload their goods, but he always pays with bearskin.

KATSIIA

[¹kat ²tsi: ja#] The female head

KATSIIA is a female head without a body that lies in a crevasse and shouts at passing hunters.

THE GIANT WOMAN *KATSIIA* would kill people whenever they made her mad. As she was only the second wife of the *angakkoq Aattaaritaa*, he decided to kill her before she did any more damage. When he tried to shoot her, she made herself very small and thin and hid behind a post in their house, but he managed to kill her in the end. He cut her up and hid her head far away from the rest of her body, but it lived on and would tell its story to anyone who cared to listen.

KIIAPPA

[²ki: ¹jap pa#] The big mask

KIIAPPA is a giant mask with arms and legs but no body or head.

It can frighten people to death by appearing in front of them, and it can possess people and make them sick by stealing their souls. When a person is possessed, their body will be covered with big bruises and they will suffer from terrible fits. If someone dies while still possessed by a *KIIAPPA*, their corpse might wake up with a scream and jump around.

KILIFFAK

[ki ¹lif fak#] The scraper

KILIFFAK is a big, long-haired creature with six—and sometimes ten—legs. It is bigger than a polar bear and has a long body due to its many legs. Its fur has a white spot on its rump; some are white all over, which makes them very beautiful and highly sought-after. It is so big that its fur can line the inside of a whole house.

It lives close to the ice cap, where it wanders around and scrapes the ground looking for food. If you kill it, you can feed a whole settlement, and the flesh will grow back on its bones twice.
If you choose to hunt it, you must be careful that it doesn't end up catching you as it runs very fast and its bite is very powerful.

A MAN HAD TURNED INTO A *QIVITTOQ* and walked inland looking for food. Once he got there he took off his *kamiik*, but then he spotted a huge *KILIFFAK* scraping the ground some distance away. At first he just sat watching it to pass the time while his *kamiik* dried out, but he was forced to flee when the *KILIFFAK* suddenly noticed him. He ran faster than a human because he was a *QIVITTOQ*, but the creature still gained on him. He jumped across a big crevice, as did the creature. But when he jumped across the next crevice, the *KILIFFAK* was so fast that it didn't see it in time, and it fell into the crevice and died.

KISERMAAQ

[ki ¹sɜm ²mɑ:q#] The lonely one

KISERMAAQ is a helper spirit that looks like a big *qajaq*. Its front opens to reveal a huge mouth filled with sharp teeth like those of a polar bear. Its mouth opens and closes like a pair of scissors, and it can shout very loudly.

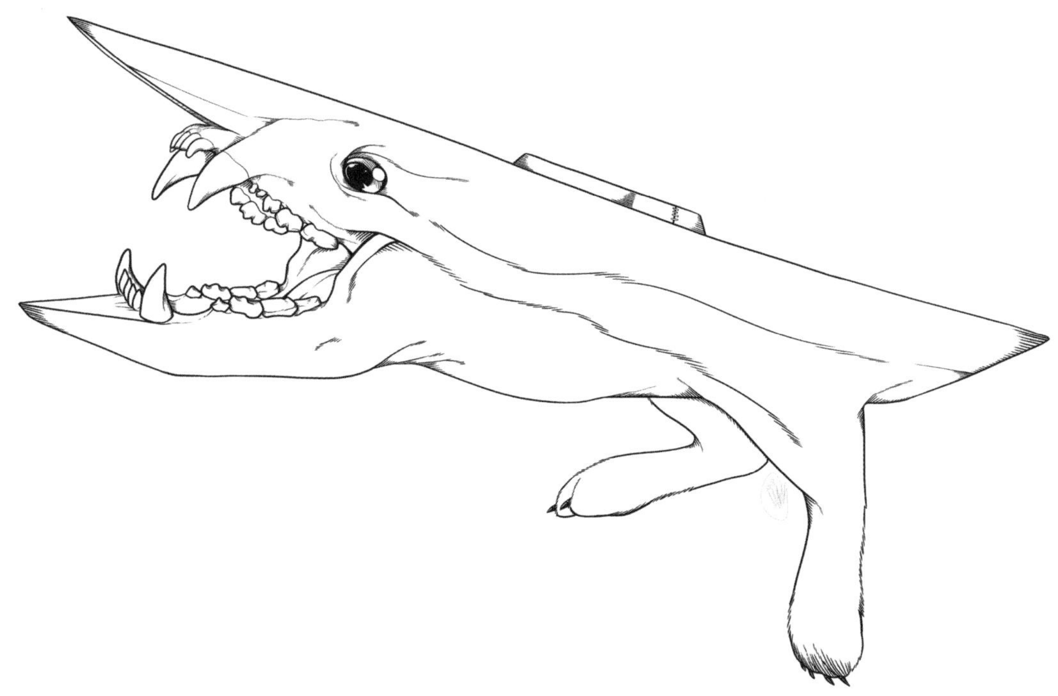

KUKIFFAAJOOQ

[ku ¹kif ²fa: ²jɔ:q#] The claw animal

KUKIFFAAJOOQ is an aggressive animal with very sharp, long claws down its back and black-and-white striped fur. When it hoots or roars, it sounds like a trumpet.

It can take down a snow bunting in flight by arching its back, jumping up, and gripping it with its claws. It hides its catch in a hole in the ground. If you are skilful, you can sneak up on it and catch it by tying its front paws together so it can't jump.

KUUPAJEEQ

[²ku: ²pa: ²jɜ:q#] Iron claws

KUUPAJEEQ is an aggressive creature with a fat belly and long iron claws on its hands and feet. The claws are so hard that a *KUUPAJEEQ* can dig holes in even the toughest granite.

They are described primarily as women, and in many stories a *KUUPAJEEQ* are also capable of giving birth to offspring just as bloodthirsty as their mothers. If they can't find a mate, they have been known to dig up an *ANNGIAQ*.

A HUNTER WAS FLEEING A *KUUPAJEEQ*, but every time he jumped across a river, it would do likewise. The hunter stopped and asked the *KUUPAJEEQ* how it was able to do that. It told him that it just drank lots of water, and the hunter asked it to demonstrate. It started to drink the water from a mountain lake, but it was unable to stop and kept drinking until it burst.

MAKAKAJUIT

[ma ka ka ju wit#] The sea people

MAKAKAJUIT are small, naked creatures who are fond of stealing all the contents of a hunter's bag or cutting the tips off his harpoons if there is any meat on them.

They sit on mountaintops and keep an eye on passing hunters so they can dive into the sea and steal their catch. They are resourceful and can take down an *IMMAP NANUA* by cutting the sinews on its paws.

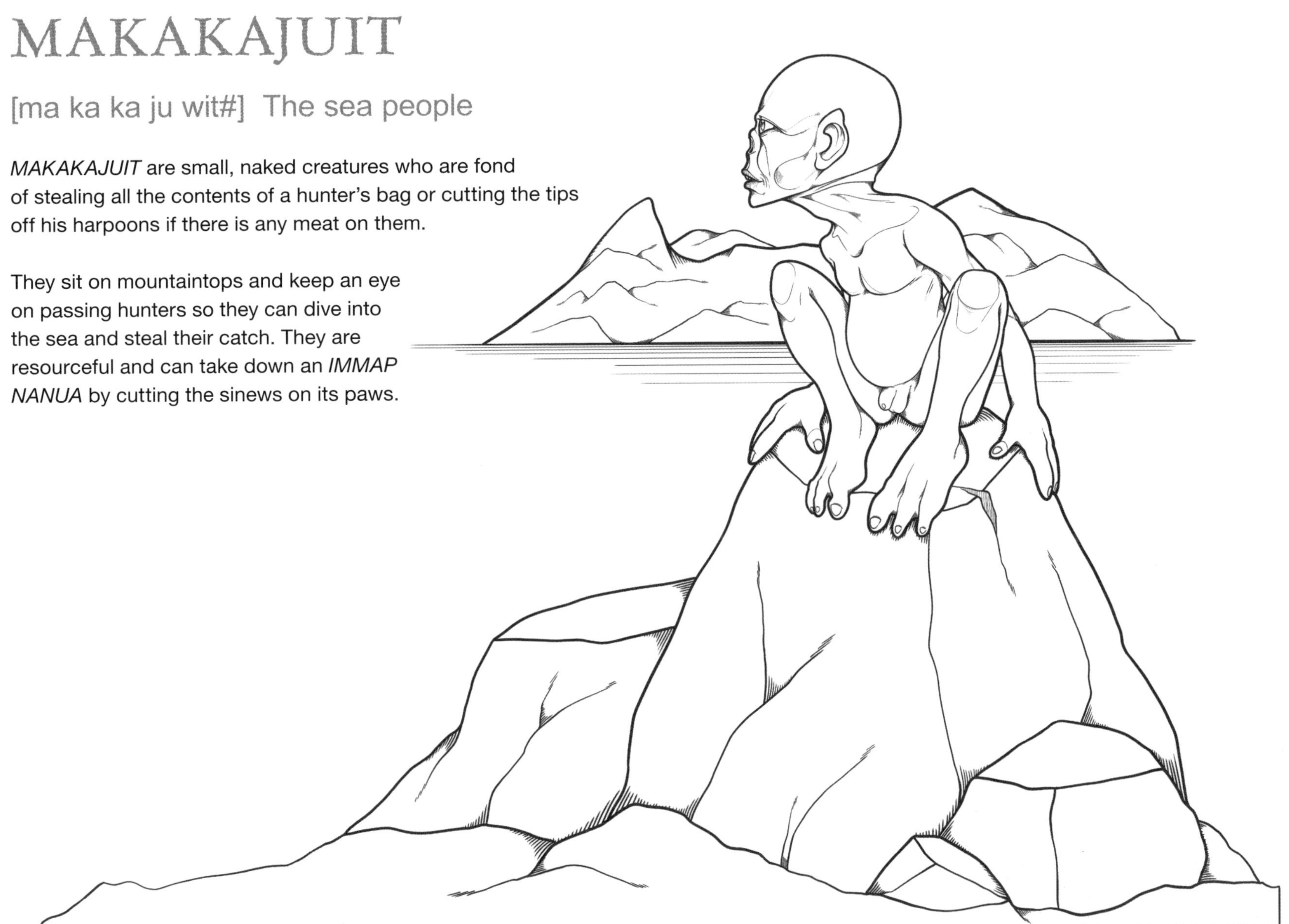

MALIINA

[ma ²li: na#] The sun

MALIINA is a beautiful young woman who wanders across the sky during the day. She only has one breast and holds a torch made from moss with which she lights up the world.

If travellers can see that the sun is setting and realize that it will be dark before they reach their destination, they can sacrifice some sinew thread to her. As the sun is female, she might busy herself plaiting the sinew and thus move more slowly across the sky. This may delay the setting sun.

ONCE UPON A TIME A BROTHER AND SISTER lived together in a big family house. Whenever they played *qaminngaarneq* at night, the brother would climb under the furs to his sister and make love to her. The sister wanted to know who lay with her at night, so one evening she rubbed her hands with soot from the lamp and made sure to smear the shoulders of her lover when he came to visit her. The next morning when the lamps were lit, the sister discovered that her lover was none other than her own brother. She grabbed her flensing knife, cut off one breast, and threw it at her brother. “Seeing that I’m so tasty, why don’t you have the rest of me!” she said. She grabbed a stick, put moss at the end of it, dipped it in train oil, lit it, and ran out the door.

She ran so fast that she took off from the earth and rose higher and higher in the sky until she turned into the sun. The brother ran after his sister, and when he saw that she had soared into the air, he grabbed his ice scraper, stuck some moss on it, and ignited it. He ran after her until he, too, rose up into the sky, where he was turned into the moon. However, as he rose, his lamp moss went out and only embers remained. He still follows his sister night after night, but has to stop every now and then to blow on the embers to keep them from going out. Every time he blows on them, sparks fly. These sparks become the stars in the sky.

NALAARSIK

[na ^{2}lɑ:s sik#] The Vega star

NALAARSIK is the big star, Vega, that tells the time during the dark period in East Greenland. He wears an *ikiaq* with white embroidery and is handy with a bow and arrow.

He is often seen with *ANINGAAQ,* whom he accompanies from the sky when they come down to visit the world of humans.

NAPPAASILAT

[¹nap ²pa: si lat#] The spirit bear

NAPPAASILAT is a big polar bear with bluish fur and a neck that is almost as wide as its body. It is most often found in inland lakes.

It can have several functions, but it acts primarily as a kind of portal for an apprentice *angakkoq* to become a full-fledged *angakkoq*. This often happens in partnership with *AAVERPAK*. In cases of illness, an *angakkoq* can become possessed by a *NAPPAASILAT* and cure the patient of their suffering.

MARATSI, AN *ANGAKKOQ*, WAS SUMMONED when a young woman was dying from an infected wound to her side. *Maratsi* took off his clothes and lay down beside her, covered by a fur. Then he let the *NAPPAASILAT* possess him and rose in the shape of a big bear. He approached the sick woman again, took a knife, cut open the infected wound and, still in the shape of the bear, licked it clean. He transformed himself back into a human being and blew on the wound, which then closed. The woman survived, and her father gave *Maratsi* a saw with an iron blade to thank him for saving his daughter.

NATTAANNGUAQ

[¹nat ²taːŋ ŋu wɑq#] The small chopper

NATTAANNGUAQ is a helper spirit for the *angakkoq Qupersimaan*. It is small, looks like a human, and lives near angelica roots.

Qupersimaan often uses *NATTAANNGUAQ* for counselling and advice: it is all-knowing and often capable of sensing the future.

NEQIKITSULIAQ

[nɜ qi ¹kit tsu li jɑq#] The gluttonous baby

NEQIKITSULIAQ is a baby with a giant stomach and big teeth who eats its parents and everyone around it.

The baby is either greedy from birth and shows this by eating the hands of the midwife on its way out of its mother or it turns into a monster later on if it thinks it is not given enough to eat. Even if you try to flee from it in an *umiaq*, it might decide to chase you by walking on water.

A BROTHER AND SISTER were being fostered by a couple whose own children didn't grow very much. When the wife had yet another baby, she decided to starve it so that there would be more food for her other children. However, her foster daughter would secretly give the baby a little food and water every now and then. The baby grew as fast as lightning, and one night everyone was woken up by the sound of the baby eating its mother. All the inhabitants of the house fled in their boat, but the two foster children were too late to get on board, and they hid under an old *umiaq*. The *NEQIKITSULIAQ* sniffed them out anyway, but the girl reached out an *ulu*, which also served as her amulet, and reminded the monster that she had fed it when no one else would. The *NEQIKITSULIAQ* left them alone and crawled on to find other victims. The two children quickly fled inland.

NERRERSUUT

[^{1}nɜχ ^{1}χɜs ^{2}su:t#] The gluttons

NERRERSUUT are greedy, big-bellied creatures who can grow so fat that they need special belts to hold in their stomachs. They are always hungry, and if they have access to food, they will eat until they can't move. When they have eaten a big meal, they rest their stomachs in hollows in the ground in order to relax and ease the pressure on their full bellies. They can move faster backward than forward and can catch a running human being despite their big bellies.

The female ones especially are said to be greedy, and if a husband of one or more *NERRERSUUT* women doesn't bring home enough meat for them, they might end up eating him. These women carry a big *ulut* so they can cut themselves some meat whenever they get hungry. Any guest who visits a *NERRERSUUT* should bring a lot of meat or they end up being dinner themselves.

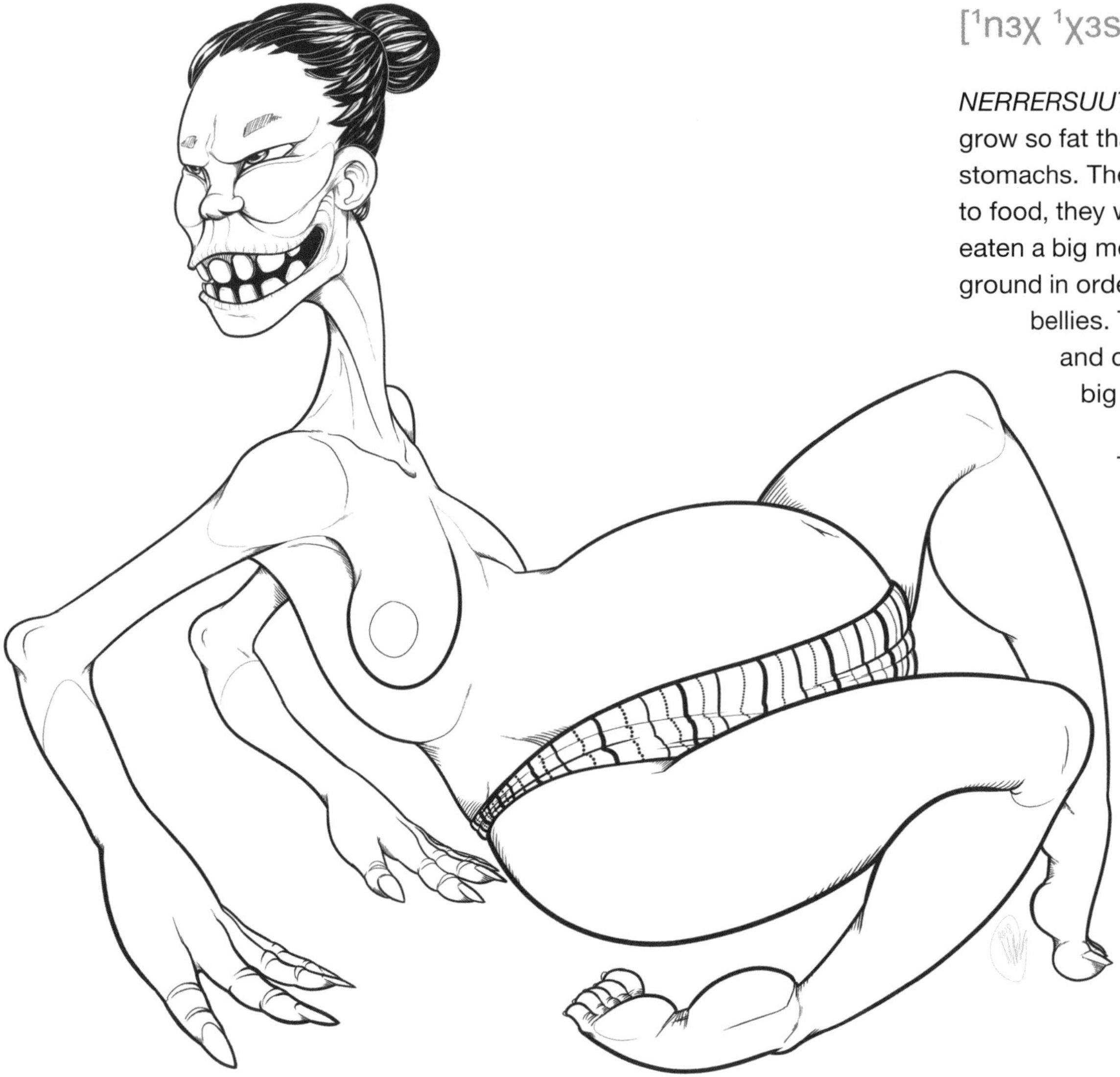

PARPALIGAMIK UNIAKATTALIK

[¹pɑp pa ¹li ɣa mik# u ni ¹kat ta lik#] The iron tail

PARPALIGAMIK UNIAKATTALIK is a human-like creature with a powerful iron tail that it swings as it walks backward toward its attackers. If its head is cut off, it will carry on grunting.

PARPALIGAMIK UNIAKATTALIK is in some stories described as having several animal qualities and is sometimes used as a draft animal, but it is mostly described as being similar to humans.

A MAN WAS ABANDONED by his wife and paddled far away, grieving. From his *qajaq* he spotted an old woman who was cooking food in front of a cabin and paddled over to greet her. She invited him to stay the night and served him meat, but he discovered that it was human flesh and declined. When he was about to go to sleep, he noticed a big bundle on the couch but thought nothing of it. During the night, he woke up to urinate and on impulse placed a big rock under his sweater, right above his heart. When he returned to the furs he slept under, he only pretended to go to sleep. Suddenly a creature with a long iron tail jumped out from under the bundle and swung his tail at the man, but he broke it on the stone. The man fled from the cabin but was chased by the old woman, wielding a big *ulu*. He made it down to his *qajaq*, where he killed her with his harpoon.

PISSAAP INUA

[¹pis ²sa:p# i nu wa#] The Lord of Strength

PISSAAP INUA is a big fox- or dog-like creature with a human face and a very long tail. It is very wise and strong, and people seek it out between the two high mountains where it lives to give them strength.

KAASSASSUK, AN ORPHANED BOY, was being bullied by the other people from his settlement. They would pick him up by his nostrils and humiliate him. He had an old foster mother who was very fond of him, and she told him to go find *PISSAAP INUA*. He went for a long walk, calling out for *PISSAAP INUA* all the time until the creature appeared. It wrapped its long tail around him and flung him into the air. As *Kaassassuk* flew through the air, his old toys fell out of his pockets, after which he suddenly felt much lighter. He went to see *PISSAAP INUA* on two other occasions and eventually grew so strong that he could easily move big boulders.

QAJARIAQ

[qa jɑ ʁi jɑq#] The giant *qajaq* man

QAJARIAQ is a giant who sits in a huge *qajaq* made from birchbark, which sometimes has a flat bottom. The giant uses an oar with a single blade to paddle. The *qajaq* itself is so deep that it would reach an ordinary man's armpits.

A *QAJARIAQ* can be seriously bloodthirsty and aggressive and has a habit of tying body parts from anyone he kills to his *qajaq*. He can cause bad weather by blowing into a small pipe, which brings about a storm.

QAMALLARLUTIK

[qa ^{1}maɬ ^{1}ɬɑɬ ɬu tsik#]
The little ones ready to jump

QAMALLARLUTIK are little people who live deep inland in small peat cabins and who can turn into ptarmigan. They can't sit still and are always delighted to have visitors.

A YOUNG WOMAN had a falling out with her parents and decided to head to the mountains to become a *QIVITTOQ*. When she had been walking for some time, she came across lots of little people who were happy to invite her to live with them. She even married one of them because she was so contented there. One day as she was cleaning the skins of earless seals that her husband had caught for her, she heard a whooshing sound behind her. When she looked around, all her new friends had disappeared and a flock of ptarmigan were flying above her. When she turned back to her skins, they had been turned into a pile of peat moss.

QAQQAT NAALAGAAT

[¹qɑq qat# ²na: la ²ɣa:t#]
The Lord of the Mountains

QAQQAT NAALAGAAT is the biggest and steepest of all the mountains and can, with the help of a skilled *angakkoq*, feed a starving settlement.

AN *ANGAKKOQ* ONCE went looking for food for his settlement with his wife and was persuaded to bring along a young boy as well. They walked for a long time until they finally reached a big mountain, where they sat down on a large, flat stone. The *angakkoq* took his stick and beat it against the stone while he mumbled some spells. Eventually his stick began to sink into the stone, where it formed a hole. He pulled out the stick, tied his *kamik* strap around it like a noose, and put it back in the hole. It looked as if he was struggling with something in the hole, and there was sweat on his brow as he tried to retrieve his stick. When he finally got it out, there were two big pieces of *mattak* in the noose. He tried again, this time using his wife's hairband, and pulled out fresh pieces of reindeer meat. The young boy couldn't wait to tell the whole settlement about their adventure, but when he ate a piece of seaweed that the *angakkoq* had passed to him, he instantly forgot everything. He didn't remember the event until many, many years later, by which time the *angakkoq* had died of old age.

QARLIMAATSOQ

[^{1}qɑɬ ɬi ^{2}ma:t tsɔq#] The ghoul

QARLIMAATSOQ is a ghoul with a black face whose body is all dried up. It usually lives in a grave. When it rises from the grave, it looks like the northern lights in the sky. It will sometimes lie screaming in its grave during a full moon. If there is a *QARLIMAATSOQ* in a grave, you may hear a buzzing sound, and if a grave has collapsed, it is said that the dead has gone for a walk.

QARLIMAATSOQ is a much sought-after helper spirit for an *angakkoq*, who makes it his helper spirit by rubbing a stone on the grave, at which point the grave will open.

QIVITTUT

[qi ¹vit tut#] Mountain wanderers

QIVITTUT are known and found across all of Greenland, in older as well as recent times. They are created when someone leaves their settlement in shame, in anger, or in grief. This person will walk far across the mountains or the ice cap in order to sever contact with all other people and live either in solitude or together with other *QIVITTUT*.

QIVITTUT are often dressed in hare or fox skin and wear *kamiik* made from twigs of different roots or leather straps. Their eyes are red, and their hair and beards are matted and often very blond or completely white. The skin on their faces has become very dark. Being touched by a *QIVITTOQ* can be very dangerous as it can cause infected wounds.

If you want to acquire magic powers as a *QIVITTOQ*, you must undergo certain trials and lose all your humanity in order to achieve total transformation. At first you must spend five days freezing to death. Once you become a *QIVITTOQ,* you can never die from the cold, and you never need to fear that you don't have a roof over your head if you can't find a cave or are unable to build a house. As a *QIVITTOQ,* you can also talk to some animals. The first animal you eat as a *QIVITTOQ* is the animal you will always sound like when you open your mouth. So if you eat a ptarmigan, you will cackle like one, and the same goes for a fox or a hare. When a woman is turned into a *QIVITTOQ*, she may at times be transformed into an *ALLAQ* and have an exceptional sense of hearing. When you achieve magic powers as a *QIVITTOQ*, you will also be capable of flying and can often be seen floating across the mountains with a tail of fire trailing behind you or breathing fire out of your mouth. When you fly, you need to tie your legs so that one is stretched out under your body so you can steer with it. If your legs are not tied, they will spread and thus lower the speed of the flying *QIVITTOQ*.

A YOUNG MAN had an aunt who didn't like his girlfriend. It made him deeply unhappy, and he went out to become a *QIVITTOQ*. The women from his settlement decided to avoid the area where he had gone missing yet were tempted by its many berries. Whenever they went there, they could hear him singing to them, but they couldn't see him. His former girlfriend cried so much that all the women started to cry with her. One day he sang that he would marry an *EQQILIK* and that his aunt would have to be contented with the family member she would now get, seeing as he had not been allowed to have the woman he loved. From that day onward, they never heard from him again.

QULLERMIUT

[[1]quɬ [1]ɬ3m mi jut#] The spirits in the sky

QULLERMIUT are spirits in the sky that try to catch *angakkoq* who are on their spirit journey. If the *QULLERMIUT* catch one, they will either kick them about like a ball or beat them with sticks until blood drips onto their drum from the spirit world.

They can be captured as helper spirits but only by people from North Greenland.

QUNGUSSUTARIAQ

[qu ¹ŋus su tɑ ʁi jɑq#] The smiling merman

QUNGUSSUTARIAQ is a smiling merman who swims up to chat to *qajaq* rowers. He carries a knife the size of a bird's wing, which he keeps hidden under the surface of the sea.

QUNGUSSUTARIAQ is very curious. He often asks about the *qajaq* rower's equipment or if he can have a present. He is quite harmless unless you smile back at him, which can make him so angry that he will curse or kill you. And if you happen to say the wrong thing to him, he will flip backward and disappear deep into the sea. At times he will surface to punish people for breaking taboos or if they have failed to admit to their *angakkoq* abilities in public. However, he has also been known to reward people and help them if they are in trouble.

A MAN AND HIS WIFE were unable to have children. The man was a great *angakkoq*, so he asked a *QUNGUSSUTARIAQ* to impregnate his wife. One night when the man and woman lay together on their couch, the wife suddenly felt something cold on her body and detected a strong smell of fish. She later gave birth to a son, who grew up to become a great *angakkoq* himself.

SASSUMA ARNAA

[^{1}sas su ma# ^{1}ɑn ^{2}na:#] Mother of the Sea

SASSUMA ARNAA is a giant woman who lives at the bottom of the sea, guarding all sea life. When people break a taboo, their transgressions turn into dirt that sticks to her skin and hair. When she gets dirty, she gets angry and stops the fish and sea mammals from swimming away from her. This creates starvation in the human world. An *angakkoq* will need to travel to the bottom of the sea to appease her and get her to release the sea life.

There are several different versions of her creation myth, her function, and explanations of where the sea life comes from. In the *Nivikka* story, she is described as a *kiffaq* who is thrown overboard on a sailing trip and whose middle fingers are chopped off. In another story, she is a small orphan girl thrown overboard with her dog because she cries too much and is useless. In this story, both her hands are cut off at the wrist. Popular oral versions (not recorded by early Greenlandic sources) tell of her fingers being chopped off joint by joint before her hands are severed and how these body parts turn into the animals of the sea.

There are likewise many different versions of the journey down to *SASSUMA ARNAA* as well as the process of cleaning her. A common feature is that once she has been cleaned, she lets the animals go. In some versions, the animals appear either from a curtain behind her couch or from her lamp, which she took with her when she sank to the bottom of the sea.

In time her function has changed, and today she has become a powerful symbol of sea pollution and climate change. She is a mainstay of Greenlandic cultural history and has been depicted by many different artists throughout Greenland over time.

NIVIKKA, A LITTLE ORPHANED GIRL, lived with a hunter and his family and worked as his *kiffaq*. The hunter had a foul temper, and he was always the first to go travelling in the summer, but one summer he hesitated, and everyone else at the settlement was scared to leave before him in case they upset him. Finally, he gave orders for the *umiaq* to be loaded, and *Nivikka* worked twice as hard as everybody else to make room for her two possessions: a dog and a lamp. Once the boat was at sea, the hunter got mad at *Nivikka* and leaped from the tiller to throw her and her possessions overboard. *Nivikka* managed to grab the gunwale and clung, terrified, to her dog but had her three middle fingers chopped off one hand. She then said goodbye to the four corners of the world, summoned all sea animals and seabirds, and sank with her dog to the bottom of the sea, where she discovered her lamp. She took her lamp and walked with her dog farther out, so far that she could see everything that was going on all over the world. There she built herself a house at the bottom of the sea. That year's hunt failed for everyone from her former settlement and it would again whenever someone broke her taboo. This would cause her to trap the animals with a bad southwesterly wind, *imarsarneq*. She would hide the animals that she had trapped in the bowl of her lamp and only release them once no one had offended her.

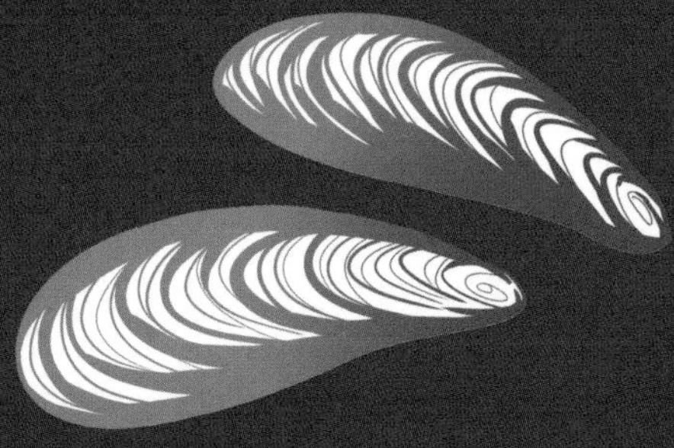

A SETTLEMENT HAD SUFFERED POOR HUNTING for a long time. The people asked their *angakkoq Uitsateqanngitseq*, who was blind, to travel to the spirit world to appease *SASSUMA ARNAA* and to ask her to release the sea creatures. *Uitsateqanngitseq* let himself be bound and for the drum to be played until he fell into a trance where his spirit left his body and flew up from the people under him. All his helper spirits accompanied him as he travelled the Path of the Dead to reach her house. He flew until he landed in front of a cascading river with three big stones in the middle, which he could use to cross the river. Unfortunately, the stones were covered by moss and very slippery, and *Uitsateqanngitseq* was very scared of jumping until his helper spirits showed him how to cross safely.

After some time, they reached the house of *SASSUMA ARNAA*, but the entrance was blocked by yet another river. With the help of his helper spirits, *Uitsateqanngitseq* once more found a safe way to cross and reach the other side. When he stood in front of the entrance, his helper spirits stopped him and said, "When you meet *SASSUMA ARNAA*, you must jump up quickly, grab her hair, and entangle your arms in it. She will be furious and try to throw you off, and if she succeeds, you will be thrown into the darkness behind her couch and suffocate." *Uitsateqanngitseq* entered the house where the river flowed the wrong way so that no animals could get out, and the bottom was filled with gravel and stone. As soon as *Uitsateqanngitseq* reached *SASSUMA ARNAA*, he quickly grabbed her hair and held on tight. While she raged, his helper spirits jumped up and whispered placatory words in her ears and told her that he had only come to cleanse her. Finally, she relaxed and let him clean her and groom her, and when she was clean again, *Uitsateqanngitseq* gathered all the dirt and threw it away. The animals began to emerge from her hair, and they smiled at the *angakkoq* as they swam past him.

Once the animals had gone, he gathered her hair in a *qilertit*, and she thanked him warmly and said, "You have made me happy because ever since you were little you have only thought deep thoughts and chosen to become an *angakkoq*. When you return to the people, you must teach them to follow my rules and taboos so that I won't be covered by dirt and grime again. Human indifference and idleness make me ugly and hideous." She gave him one of her hairs, which she wrapped around his arm, and bade him farewell. As *Uitsateqanngitseq* walked back through the passage, the river was flowing the right way out of the house, and the bottom was covered with fine, white sand. He returned to the human world, told them *SASSUMA ARNAA*'s instructions, and let them know that they had caused her trouble. The people all repented and promised to mend their ways so that she would not be covered by human dirt again.

SERMILISSUAQ

[ˈsɜm mi ˈlis su waq#] The bear covered in ice

SERMILISSUAQ is a giant polar bear formed by an ice mountain and completely covered in icicles. It is very dangerous to people as it feeds on human flesh.

It comes wandering either from the water when the ice cap melts or from hollows in the mountains when the sun comes out. Its breath is so heavy that it can cover the whole landscape in fog.

TWO TERRIFIED HUNTERS RETURNED to their settlement because while out ice fishing they had come across a *SERMILISSUAQ*, which they had seen under the water near an ice mountain. A young man made himself a bow and some arrows and went off to hunt it. He made a hole in the ice with a chisel close to the ice mountains, and when he looked down into the hole, he could see *SERMILISSUAQ* walking on that part of the ice mountain, which lay under water. He started to whistle, and soon the bear poked its big head up through the hole in the ice, but it could not get the rest of its body out. The young man made the hole bigger and bigger until finally all of the bear could get out, whereupon the young man plunged his chisel into the eyes of the bear before it had emerged fully, and he ran around in circles until the bear that nearly caught him fell down dead.

SERMIP INUA

[ˈsɜm mip# i nu wa#] The Lord of the Ice Cap

SERMIP INUA has a human face and the skeletal body of a sheep or a dog.

It has a cave on the ice cap, and the entrance to its cave is a crack in the glacier ice surrounded by broken stones. Anyone who wants to become an *angakkoq* will go there to visit it.

AATTAARITAA WENT TO SEE *SERMIP INUA*, and when he reached its cave, he hid his mouth behind the edge of his hood, slipped one arm out of his anorak, and pointed it downward. He called out, "*SERMIP INUA*, come out! I want to be an *angakkoq*!" but lost his nerve and fled. The second time he tried it, he managed to overcome his fear, and then he was swallowed up by *SERMIP INUA*. When he came round, he had achieved clarity of vision and could see all of his settlement and all the people who lived there whenever he closed his eyes. He also gained the ability to see seals swimming under water when he was out hunting, which made him a very successful hunter.

TARRAJAARSUIT

[ˈtɑχ χa ˈjɑs su wit#] The shadows

TARRAJAARSUIT are semi-invisible creatures who struggle to take on physical shapes. When they finally manage it, they are so fragile that they might burst and turn into slime.

They live in houses just like people and are very hospitable to travellers. They can also serve as helper spirits to an *angakkoq*.

A YOUNG WOMAN had walked far inland, and she came across a small house with three windows. She looked through one of the windows and saw a seal being flayed, but she couldn't see any people, only shadows. She felt someone nudge her but couldn't see anyone when she turned around. Then she heard a voice inviting her in, but once inside she still could see nothing but shadows. Suddenly an old married couple were lying on one of the couches next to her, and she lay down beside them. A dish of meat was passed around, but apart from the old couple, she couldn't see anyone eating—only that the plate was cleared. She went to bed but woke up in the middle of the night when she felt something slimy next to her. She realized that there was also lots of blood. It was the old couple who had burst from overeating, and the young woman fled the house in terror.

TIMERSIIT

[tsi ¹mɜs ²si:t#] Inland inhabitants from East Greenland

TIMERSIIT are human-like giants who live deep inland in East Greenland, close to or even on the ice cap. They can paddle *qaannat* but prefer to harpoon big seals and narwhals from the shore. They also like to hunt reindeer.

TIMERSIIT are usually friendly as they trade with and visit humans, but they will sometimes steal human children and raise them as their own, and they have been known to rape people. A few are so dangerous that they attack and rip out the guts of the people who visit them, so you should take great care if you bump into them. They also have unique, magical powers and can summon and walk on fog, which is how they get from island to island if they are going on a long journey or to fetch whales in the sea if they can't reel them in. They can also summon animals with a special call. The doors to their houses are big stones, often three leaning together, and they frequently have curtains of pearls, stones, or teeth in front of the entrances to warn against trespassing. *TIMERSIIT* wives are skilled seamstresses and can make a garment that will fit perfectly from just a quick glance at you.

A MAN WAS OUT PADDLING HIS *qajaq* but was captured by a *TIMERSEQ* woman carrying a child in an *amaat*, although he desperately tried to paddle in the other direction. The woman dragged him ashore and had sex with him, after which the man became impotent. He was impotent for the rest of his life right until the day he died, when his dead body got an erection.

TOORNAARSUK

[²tɔːn ²nɑːs suk#] Lord of the Helper Spirits

TOORNAARSUK is the Lord of the Helper Spirits and is the strongest helper spirit an *angakkoq* can have. For that reason, it is the one most often used by an *angakkoq* in very tricky situations.

A *TOORNAARSUK* doesn't have a single, specific appearance; it varies from *angakkoq* to *angakkoq*. These helper spirits are, however, often good swimmers and very strong. All *TOORNAARSUIT* have one thing in common: they rule over the other helper spirits.

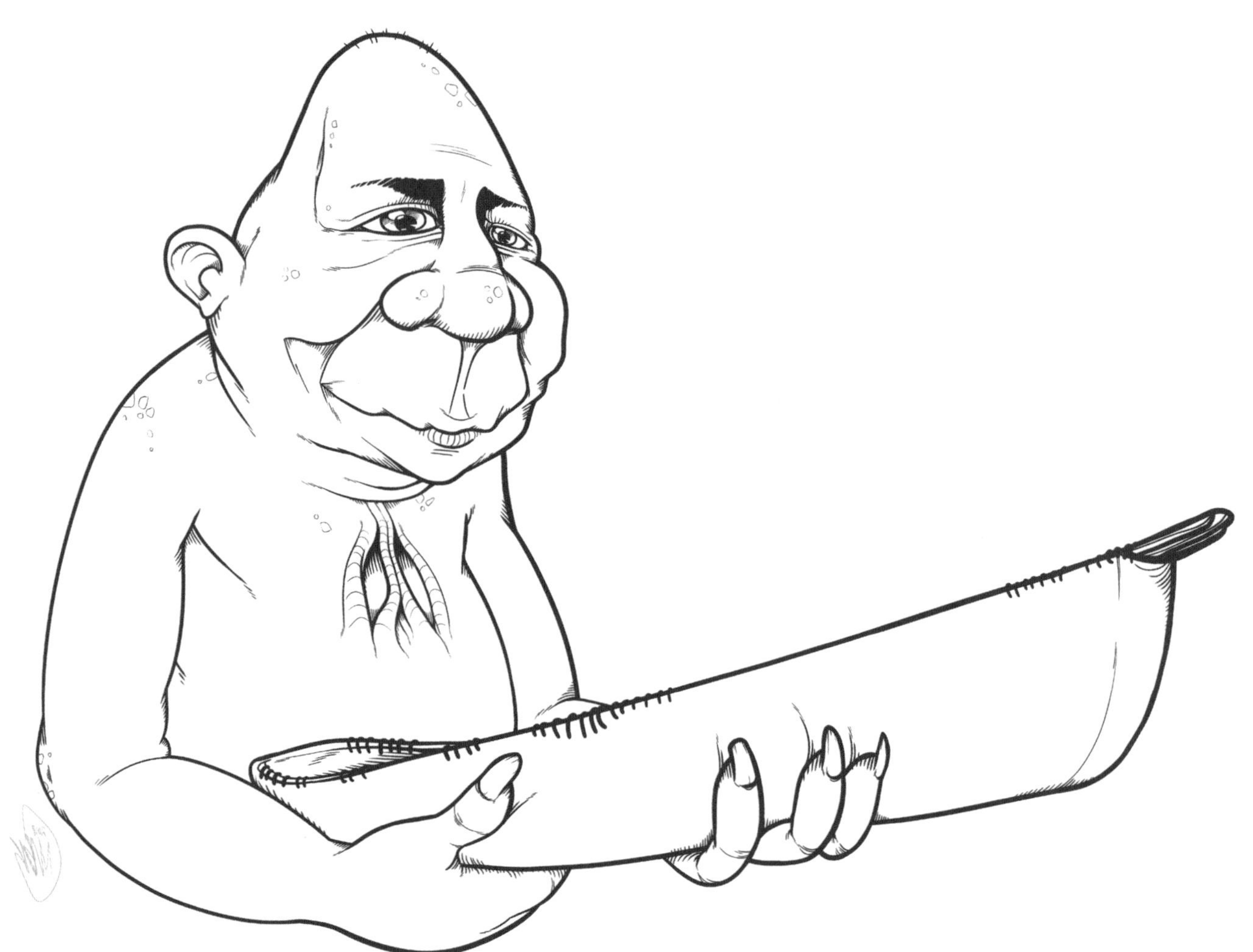

TUNIT

[tu nit#]
Inland inhabitants from West Greenland

TUNIT are human-like giants who live on the *nunataq* of the ice cap or deep inland on the peaks of tall mountains. They can grow so big that they can scoop up an *umiaq* with one hand and they have blowholes in their chests. They speak a kind of childish language when they interact with people, and they have a preference for eating hare and fox testicles, which they call "crunchy balls."

They are rather more aggressive than their east coast cousins, the *TIMERSIIT*, but they will occasionally trade with humans or even marry them.

A *TUNEQ* AND AN *INORUSEQ* were both watching a seal from a distance. The *INORUSEQ* reached it first, but the *TUNEQ* insisted that he had seen it first. The *INORUSEQ* stomped towards the seal with his tail flapping up and down; he snatched the seal and bashed it so hard against the ground that everything shook. The *TUNEQ* continued to claim that he had seen the seal first and that it belonged to him. A fight ensued, and the *TUNEQ* swung the *INORUSEQ* around and threw him into the air, but the *INORUSEQ* managed to curl up and didn't get hurt. The *INORUSEQ* then did the same to the *TUNEQ*, who didn't have time to curl up and was beaten so badly that he vomited blood and got dizzy. The *INORUSEQ* picked up the seal and left, and the *TUNEQ* had to skulk home with his tail between his legs in shame.

TUPILAK

['tu pi lak#] The avenger

A *TUPILAK* is made up of parts from animals and people and is used to take revenge. It can look very different depending on the parts from which it is made, and it can have many different abilities. But what all *TUPILAAT* have in common is the terrifying and the grotesque; they are often skinny or skeletal, which makes the thought of being chased by one almost as frightening as actually seeing one. A few *TUPILAAT,* such as *UERSAT INUAT,* have specific abilities.

You can bring a *TUPILAK* to life in many ways, but the starting point is often the same: You gather different parts of animals and people; body parts of dead newborn babies are particularly sought-after. The parts are placed by a river and covered with moss, after which spells are said over them. As soon as the *TUPILAK* starts to come alive, it must suckle its maker's genitals so it can grow and become big and dangerous. Once it is big enough, its maker will return it to the river and tell it on whom to take revenge. A skilled *angakkoq* can protect themselves against a *TUPILAK*, but to chase away a *TUPILAK* or make it go back to its maker is no easy task. It requires not only an experienced *angakkoq* but also several helper spirits. If a *TUPILAK* is sent back, it will turn on its maker, so think twice before you take revenge.

Today we know *TUPILAAT* best as carved figures found around Greenland; they are a development of the first visualizations of the much-feared avenging animals. The carved modern *TUPILAAT* vary just as much as the creatures that have been brought to life to take revenge.

A SETTLEMENT WAS TROUBLED BY A *TUPILAK* in the shape of a bear when it was discovered that the ground under one house had been dug away. The people called for a skilled *angakkoq*, who saw the bear in a vision and tried to kill it with assistance from the helper spirits. But the *TUPILAK* kept getting away. The people called for another *angakkoq*, who was also a talented drum dancer, and the *angakkoq* started dancing and drumming. The *angakkoq* asked the helper spirit to find a lance that lay at the front of an *umiaq*. The helper spirit speared the *TUPILAK* with the lance but managed only to wound it. The furious *TUPILAK* tried to catch the helper spirit, but just as it was about to, it collapsed and died from its injuries.

Modern *TUPILAAT*
carved from bone or tusk

Traditional *TUPILAK* made
from a dead seal and a child skull

Traditional *TUPILAK* made from animal parts

UERSAT INUAT

[u ¹wɜs sat# ¹i nu wat#]
The Lord of the Illegitimate

UERSAT INUAT is a hermaphroditic spirit that can be a helper spirit, act as a *TUPILAK,* and help an *angakkoq* get revenge. It is skinny, often with several skeletal body parts, with a *qilertit*, a long, erect penis, and at times also female sexual characteristics.

UERSAT INUAT lives in a deep gorge and is summoned as a helper spirit by rubbing a large block of granite. When it appears, it will hiss and whistle. *UERSAT INUAT* may also visit an apprentice *angakkoq* to force them to reveal and use their powers as it can be dangerous to conceal them. If the *angakkoq* refuses to do so, the *UERSAT INUAT* might rape them, just as it will use rape as a weapon when taking revenge on someone.

A FEMALE *ANGAKKOQ* was bitter because the man she had originally been in love with didn't want her. This was despite her ending up marrying another great *angakkoq*. In her rage, she sent an *UERSAT INUAT* after the man, but he continued to live on, unharmed and unaffected. She then started to fear that *UERSAT INUAT* would come after her instead and refused to go outside alone. One evening as she lay down on her couch to sleep with her back against the wall, she felt the tip of its penis dig into her back. She started to scream and woke up everyone in the house. The other inhabitants saw a dark, lumpy thing stir in the place where she was sleeping. They told this to her husband, but he was busy with other things, and she disappeared unnoticed out of the house and into the night. When the rest of the inhabitants realized that she was gone, they went looking for her and found her with her trousers pulled down around her ankles, raped to death by the *UERSAT INUAT*.

UMIARISSAT

[u mi jɑ ¹ʁis sat#] The *umiaq* people

UMIARISSAT are groups of warriors with shiny weapons, who wear big hats and have bushy beards. They wink with vertical eyes. They come disguised as bearded seals, harp seals, and hooded seals, and when they reach the shore, they turn into human-like creatures in a big *umiaq* and attack settlements.

When they have finished their attack or if the inhabitants scare them off, they run away and jump back into the sea, where they turn into seals the moment they touch the water. If you notice the *UMIARISSAT* heading for your settlement, you can pour old urine along the shore where they land or head deep into the mountains and glare at them menacingly while you cut peat. Both methods are said to keep them at bay.

TWO BROTHERS LIVED on either side of a big river. Their mother lived with one of them. One evening she went to relieve herself, and while she was squatting down, she saw the *UMIARISSAT* arrive at full speed but grew so scared that she was unable to move. The *UMIARISSAT* butchered everyone in the house and got away by jumping back into the water and turning into seals. The terrified old woman ran to her second son. They got an *angakkoq* to track the attackers to the ice cap and went off to take revenge on the murderers.

SHAMANS, WITCHES, AND WITCHCRAFT

Robin Fenrir Mansa Hillestrøm

Greenlandic shamans, *angakkut*, were very important figures in pre-Christian society. There were many renowned shamans, such as *Maratsi*, *Missuarniannga*, *Sanimuinnaq*, and *Akku*, whose names are still spoken in hushed voices today. Who were they and what did they do? First here is an overview of what an *angakkoq*'s role was not.

Angakkut were important figures—but they weren't the only ones

In the basic social unit of Greenlandic society, the small family group, it was the eldest man of sound mind who made major decisions. An older woman with strong sons could also wield great influence. In large communal houses, called longhouses, where many families lived, the most respected hunter made decisions about joint concerns. When out on a hunt, however, the most skilful hunter of the animal being hunted would be in command. So a different hunter could be in charge depending on whether it was a hunt for whale, seal, walrus, polar bear, or reindeer. Outside the family group, or the longhouse, justice was served through either revenge killings or fearsome song duels, where the two parties would deliver mighty head-butting blows to each other while singing rehearsed, insulting songs.

Angakkut did not have a monopoly on magic

Magic was desired by all Inuit. Spells could sometimes be bought from wise elders or received as a gift in return for a notable kindness, favour, or duty completed. A spell was a very personal thing and, once exchanged, would be useless to its original owner.

Any self-respecting man or woman would also have several protective amulets—anything from a figure of a cormorant powerful enough to chase away the terrible *TUPILAAT* to a seal skull capable of hiding an entire *umiaq*.

Women were also *angakkut*

By far the most—and mightiest—shamans were men. However, from both historical research and oral tradition, there is evidence of great female shamans as well, such as *Ineqinnavaat* from Upernavik. Another example of a female shaman from the oral tradition is the story of the widow *Illutsiak*'s young daughter. When the hunt failed, *Illutsiak*'s daughter journeyed to the bottom of the sea to placate the feared *SASSUMA ARNAA*, Mother of the Sea. Once *SASSUMA ARNAA* was cleansed and appeased, the ice broke up and the young woman returned. As payment for her services to the community, *Illutsiak*'s daughter received half a harp seal.

Angakkut were not rare

Though researchers disagree on exact numbers, it is thought that as many as twenty percent of men and five percent of women were *angakkut* in some form or another. Of these, only a few were recognized as great shamans, *angakkorsuit*, and even fewer as truly great shamans, *angakkuvissuit*.

Not everyone believed them

There are quite a few stories of Inuit who either didn't believe in or ridiculed the powers of *angakkut*. This behaviour could not be ignored because it could lead to the *angakkoq* losing their powers. The accounts usually describe the *angakkoq* revealing the terrible fire at the centre of the *angakkoq*'s art and concluded with the disbeliever requiring a change of pants ...

Angakkuuneq was a skill, not a profession

All Inuit were active members of the family group in pre-Christian Greenland—including *angakkut*—which meant that all men were expected to know how to hunt, and all women were expected to know how to flense an animal carcass, sew, and cook. In addition to these expected skills, having magical abilities was obviously an advantage. Payment for an *angakkoq's* services was not meant to support full-time *angakkut*, but rather because the art of summoning was highly prized, payment was a symbolic reciprocity for the *angakkut* and their *toornat*, or helper spirits—a favour for a favour.

An *angakkoq* was therefore not just an *angakkoq* but also someone's father, mother, sister, cousin, or other family member. Some *angakkut* were respected for being great hunters; others were useless hunters who nonetheless were feared for their magical abilities. Others were not so different from ordinary people; they had limited magical abilities because they lacked skill, had failed their training, or had never acquired more than a single helper spirit.

Angakkuuneq is not about witchcraft

The art of the shaman, *angakkuuneq*, and witchcraft, *ilisiinneq*, were often confused by European visitors and missionaries, who are the source for most written accounts. From a Christian point of view, shamanism and witchcraft looked like devil worship and paganism, but *angakkuuneq* and *ilisiinneq* were, in fact, very different.

An *angakkoq*'s special skill was spirit summoning—the ability to peer into the other world, and the ability to speak and negotiate with the spirits. *Ilisiinneq*, on the other hand, was the ability to hurt other people by means of magic. To be a good *angakkoq,* you needed to know about both *angakkuuneq* and *ilisiinneq*. An *ilisiitsoq,* or witch, on the other hand, did not need to know how to summon spirits to work their craft. Even though the use of *ilisiinneq* against others was greatly feared and frowned upon, it seems that most older people had some skill with this darker art.

Ilisiinneq could be used both to defend oneself against the evil intentions of other *ilisiitsut*, and to harm others. The latter, active use of *ilisiinneq* was very risky because if a spell failed for one reason or another or if the intended target's magical powers were too strong, spells tended to turn on the caster.

Witchcraft was only seen as a problem if it had actually been used against another person—or if a person was blamed for doing so. It wasn't uncommon for an older person (most often a woman) to be pointed out as the guilty *ilisiitsoq* behind an accident, an unexplained death, childlessness, or a failed hunt. They would then either be killed in retaliation or publicly executed by angry relatives.

So what could an *angakkoq* do?

The old Greenlandic world view was magical, mystical, and full of souls and spirits. Every human had to live by the many magical prohibitions and taboos, then arm themselves with all the spells and powerful amulets they could lay their hands on for the rest. *Angakkut*, on the other hand, could be hired to gaze into the unknown and give answers as well as solutions: "Why am I ill? Why is the hunt so bad? Why can't I have children? Where is the harpoon tip that disappeared from my house?"

An *angakkoq* could also, it was believed, affect the cruel and mighty natural world. The journey to *SASSUMA ARNAA* to make the ice break up was a recurring ritual, as was the journey to the spirit of winds, *ASIAQ*, to make the rains fall or to stop a prolonged snowfall.

Last but not least, spirit summoning was excellent entertainment! A skilled *angakkoq*'s spirit summoning was exciting to watch, and on the *angakkoq*'s part, it was an opportunity to increase power and prestige. In other words, the business required a fair amount of showmanship. *Angakkut* would also perform a summoning on their own initiative (to acquire a new *toornaq*, for example) and if the spectators were impressed by the performance, it could be considered a success.

There were both great and small *angakkut*

Qilaneq, which was a kind of spirit fishing, was in contrast a much less demanding technique: a string is attached to a person's head, with a stick tied to the string. This method didn't yield any great fame, didn't require helper spirits, and could only provide a "yes" or "no" answer to the questions asked.

"Lying covered, on your back" was real spirit summoning. During this ritual, it was possible to acquire new helper spirits as well as give the crowd a proper show.

Ilimmarneq was the highly regarded and coveted ability to fly. Only the very best could do it. The stories are full of accounts of mighty *angakkut* travelling to distant lands and places by means of this power. An alternative to flying was hovering or gliding, which a skilled *angakkoq* would use to travel underground to the Subterranean Ones.

Just as powerful and prestigious as spirit flight was the mystical *poorsinnaleq* or *puulik*, which could only be obtained by surviving being thrown across the sea by a giant polar bear and a giant walrus. Mastering both this ability and spirit flight was preferable, of course, but only very few did.

How one became an *angakkoq*

Angakkoq training could begin in many different ways. In some stories, it was an *angakkoq* parent or other adult who began the training by, for example, performing special rituals over an infant child. In others, it was the spirits or the supernatural creatures themselves who made contact with an angry child, and from this first contact, the child might become an *angakkoq*. This stems from the pre-Christian belief that spirits would be drawn to an angry child, which is also why European visitors remarked on how gentle (or lax, in their view) child-rearing was among the Inuit. Spirits were fickle and powerful things, so unwanted attention was best avoided.

From then on, the training would happen in secret, but the exact shape and order of events vary greatly in the stories. Some paid for or were given instruction from an experienced *angakkoq*; others learned in solitude among the spirits. What they all had in common was that they went through a special initiation alone as an essential part of their training. A version of this event that is often mentioned is meeting *NAPPAASILAT*, the spirit bear.

An aspiring *angakkoq* would go inland to a lake and work themself into a trance. This could, for instance, be done by means of the *angakkoq*'s small, round stone, which was rubbed against a larger stone. If the student were skilled and persistent enough, the spirit bear would at last come and overpower him amid great pain and terror. When the young *angakkoq* awoke, he would be naked as a newborn, but he would have the *qaamaneq*, or inner fire, and therefore also the ability to see the invisible.

When the *angakkoq* had proceeded far enough in his training, it was important to go through the next initiation in public. The young *angakkoq* declared their powers to prove that they weren't just an *ilisiitsoq*, and it was then possible for others to determine if they were any good.

An aspiring *angakkoq*'s powers were measured by how powerful and plentiful their helper spirits, or toornat, were. In Missuarniannga's tale of his own career, he describes the many terrible spirits that he met. When he had survived an encounter with the same spirit three times, he could have the spirit as a *toornaq*. The mightiest and most important of all helper spirits was TOORNAARSUK, of which an *angakkoq* only had one.

What happened during a spirit summoning?

There are only a few sources for *angakkut* secrets. This was precisely because they were secrets, and if they weren't kept secret, the helper spirits might get angry and leave the *angakkoq*. Fortunately for posterity, baptized Christian *angakkut* and their descendants (such as Kârale Andreassen) could freely talk about them. Similarly, there are a few descriptions from researchers and explorers who had witnessed a spirit summoning first-hand.

The spirit summoning typically began with the inhabitants of the settlement gathering in a communal house, whereupon doors and windows were covered with stiff hides. Depending on the *angakkoq*'s power, they could be laid on the bench, covered by a pelt, or tied up to go on a spirit flight dressed only in underwear (or an *ikiaq* and boots if they were going on a gliding journey underground to visit the Subterranean Ones).

The lamps were put out—only the very mightiest *angakkut* in the old stories could spirit-summon in the light as an expression of their enormous power. For regular mortals, rituals were always in the dark. This of course gave an *angakkoq* an opportunity to build drama, such as making the *qilaat* beat without (apparently) touching it.

The *angakkoq* would begin, after some time in darkness, a trance with plaintive sighs, moaning, and snorting. And then the spirits would come.

The first to show up were often *qimarratit* such as *AMU* and *AAJUMAAQ*, who would scare the spectators out of their minds, setting the mood and warming up the crowd.

The *angakkoq*'s spirit could now leave their body and journey to the other side while a helper spirit remained behind. In addition to looking after the *angakkoq*'s body, this helper spirit could also inform the spectators of what was happening to their *angakkoq*. The stories that the creatures in this book are based on are full of the incredible adventures of travelling *angakkut*. If an *angakkoq* were particularly good, they would be able to travel all the way to *Akilineq*, the land on the other side of the ocean, where everything is strange and men and beasts are gigantic.

Or an *angakkoq* could go to *ANINGAAQ* or *SASSUMA ARNAA* to clean up after mankind's breaking of taboos, or to the dead in the sky who eat only ravens, or to the dead at the bottom of the sea who live well. An *angakkoq* could meet departed relatives or, if careless, be caught on the way by *AMAARSISARTOQ,* who presented a particular danger to *angakkut* on spirit flights.

And if the *angakkoq* were skillful and tenacious enough, they could return to their body with answers and mystical knowledge, sometimes bloody and exhausted—but alive.

ALTERNATIVE NAMES AND SPELLINGS

GREENLAND'S REGIONS

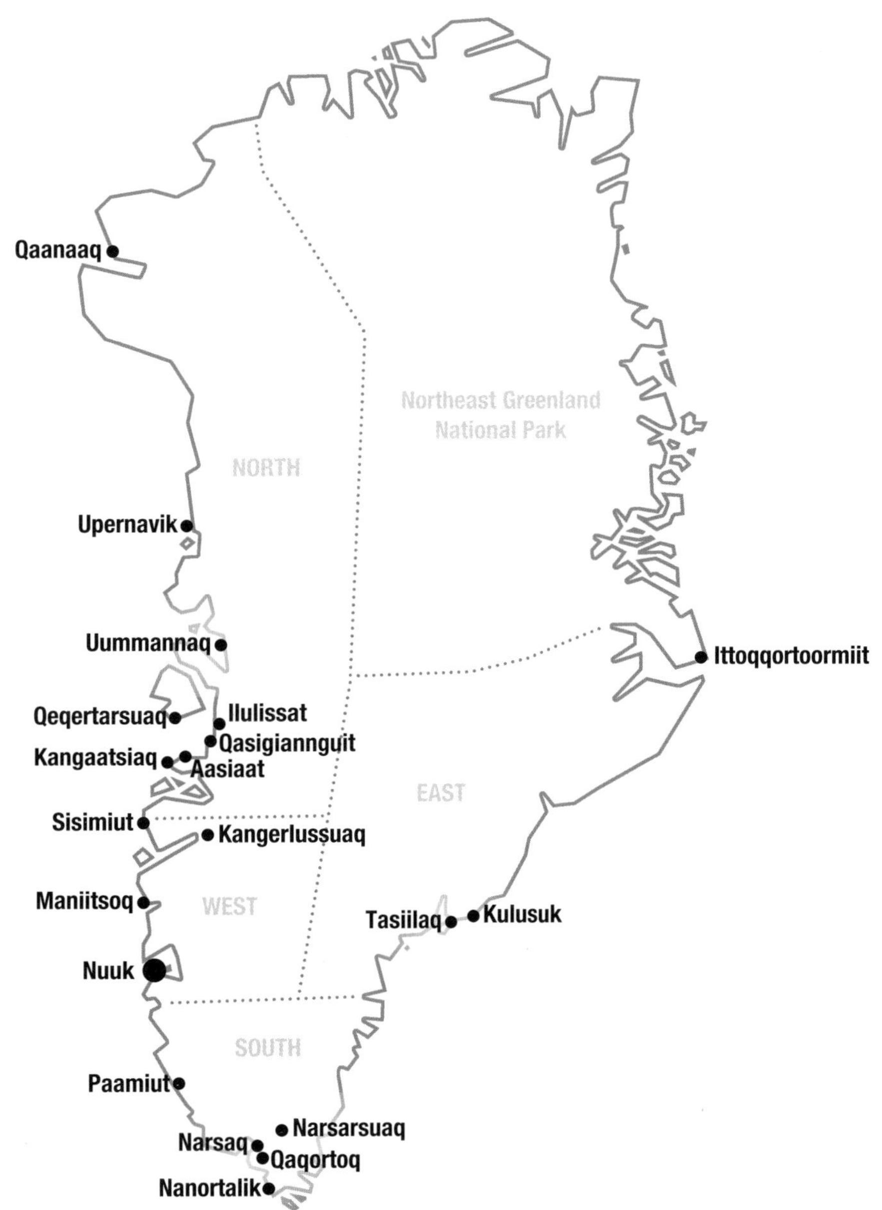

NAME	ALTERNATIVE NAMES AND SPELLINGS	REGION
AAJUMAAQ	AJUMAAQ/AAJUMAQ/AJUMAK/ÂJUMÂK	East Greenland
AASSIK	AASSIK/ÂGSSIK/AUSSIK/QULLIGIASUAQ/QULLUGIARSUAQ/QUPERDLUGESSUAQ	South/West/North Greenland
AAVERPAK	AAVERPAK/AAFFAFFAQ	East/South/West/North Greenland
AJAQQISAAQ		East Greenland
AKUEQQUTIT		East Greenland
ALLAQ		South Greenland
ALLIARUTSIT		East/South/West/North Greenland
AMAARSISARTOQ	AMAARSINIOOQ/AMÂRSINIÔQ/AMÂSISORTOQ/AMÂGAIAT	West Greenland
AMAROQ	AMAROOQ/AMAROK	West/North Greenland
AMU	AMO/AMOORTORTOQ	East Greenland
ANGIUT		East Greenland
ANINGAAQ	QAAMMAT/QAAMMATIP INUA	East/South/West/North Greenland
ANNGIAQ	ALUSSUGAQ/KIGULERAK	East/South/West/North Greenland
AQAJARORMIORSIORTOQ	AQAJARORSIORPUA	East Greenland
ARPATTUT	ARPATTAASIMASUT	West Greenland
ASIAQ	ASIAK	East Greenland
ASSAGISSAT	ASAGISAT	East Greenland
EQALUSSUAQ	EQALUGSSUAQ	South/North Greenland
ERLAVEERSINIOOQ	ERDLAVÊRSISSOQ/ERVLUARAINIARK/NALIGATEQ/NALIKÀTEQ/NALIKKATTEEQ	South/West Greenland
EQQILLIT		East/South/West/North Greenland
EQUNGASOQ	EQINGALEQ/ERQINGASEQ	East Greenland
IGALILIK		West/North Greenland
IKKIILLINEQANNGEQQISSAARTOQ		West/East Greenland
IKUSIK	IKUSIMIAQ	West Greenland
ILLUKOQ	ILLUINNAQ	West Greenland
IMMAP NANUA		East Greenland
INNERSUIT & ALLIARUTSIT	ALLIARUTSIT/ALLIARMIUT	East/South/West/North Greenland
INNERSUIT TAARTAAT		East Greenland
INORROOQ	INORROORTOQ	West Greenland
INORUTSIT		East/South/West/North Greenland
INUARAKASIK	INIVARAQ	South Greenland
INUARULLIKKAT		East/North Greenland
INUSSUAQ SAARNGIINNAQ		West Greenland
ISEQQAT		South/West/North Greenland

NAME	ALTERNATIVE NAMES AND SPELLINGS	REGION
ITTUKU	ITTUKO/ILLUKU	East Greenland
KATSIIA	KATSIJA/KATSIIJA/KATSIIAARARSIVASIK	South Greenland
KIIAPPA	KIAPA	East Greenland
KILIFFAK	KILIVFAK/ATALIK	East/South/West/North Greenland
KISERMAAQ	KISERTULIK/KIISARTULIK	South/North Greenland
KUKIFFAAJOOQ	KUKIGFÂJÔQ/KUKISSOQ/KUKISSOUK/KUKISOUK	East/South Greenland
KUUPAJEEQ	KOPAJAQ/QUPAJAQ	East Greenland
MAKAKAJUIT	MAKAKAJUVIT	East Greenland
MALIINA		East/West/North Greenland
NALAARSIK	NELAARSIK/NILAARSEQ/NILAARSIK/NELÂRSIK	East Greenland
NAPPAASILAT		East Greenland
NATTAANNGUAQ		East Greenland
NEQIKITSULIAQ	NERRIKITSULIAQ	East/South/West/North Greenland
NERRERSUUT	NERRERSIUVIT/NERRERSÛJÛT/NAARRAAJIIT/NARRAJOK	East Greenland
PARPALIGAMIK UNIAKATTALIK		South/East/North Greenland
PISSAAP INUA		West Greenland
QAJARIAQ		South/West/North Greenland
QAMALLARLUTIK		West Greenland
QAQQAT NAALAGAAT		West Greenland
QARLIMAATSOQ		South/East Greenland
QIVITTUT		East/South/West/North Greenland
QULLERMIUT	QALAK	East Greenland
QUNGUSSUTARIAQ	QUNGUSSUTARIARSUAQ/QUJAAVAARSUK	West/North Greenland
SASSUMA ARNAA	IMMAP UKUAA/IMMAP NAALAGAA/NIVIKKA	East/South/West/North Greenland
SERMILISSUAQ	NANOQ SERMILIK	South/West Greenland
SERMIP INUA		South Greenland
TARRAJAARSUIT	TARRARJAARSUIT/TARAJUATJAK/TARAJUADAT	East/West/North Greenland
TIMERSIIT	TIMERSÊK/TIMERSÊQ/TIMERSSEQ	East Greenland
TOORNAARSUK	TORNARSSUK/TOORNARSUK/TORNAT NALAGAAT	East/West Greenland
TUNIT		East/South/West/North Greenland
TUPILAK		East/South/West/North Greenland
UERSAT INUAT	UVERSAT INUAT/UERSAK/UISAQ/UVERSSAK	East/West/North Greenland
UMIARISSAT		East/West/North Greenland

GLOSSARY

Aasivik	summer camp
Akilineq	place name that means what lies across the sea or the mythical country across the sea
Amaat	baby carrier; female's fur coat with room for a baby at the back
Ammassak (sing.) **Ammassat (pl.)**	capelins; fish that swim in big shoals and are caught in large numbers
Angakkoq (sing.) **Angakkut (pl.)**	shaman
Angakkorsuaq **Angakkuvissuaq** **Angakkuvissuit**	a major shaman could advance to become an *angakkorsuaq* (big shaman) or *angakkuvissuaq* (even bigger shaman)
Angakkuuneq	shamanism; the art of the shaman
Ikiaq	anorak made from intestines. Greenland's answer to a raincoat. Made of clean seal intestines sewn together to an anorak
Ilimmarneq	spirit flight or spirit journey. Undertaken by an *angakkoq* when a bad spirit needs to be found or the sick cured
Ilisiinneq	witchcraft; the ability to hurt other people using magic
Ilisiitsoq (sing.) **Ilisiitsut (pl.)**	witch; someone who uses witchcraft or magic to cause harm
Imarsarneq	strong southwesterly wind
Kamik (sing.) **Kamiit (pl.)**	footwear. Boots made from tanned leather; can be long or short
Kiffaq	servant girl, servant, or maid
Mattak	raw whale skin and blubber, regarded as a delicacy
Nunataq	or nunatak; a mountain that sticks out of the ice cap
Poorsinnaleq	"with a bag"; a kind of spirit journey where a shaman transitions from apprentice to full-fledged shaman
Puulik	"chrysalis"; a kind of spirit journey where a shaman transitions from apprentice to full-fledged shaman

Qajaq (sing.) **Qaannat (pl.)**	kayak. Vessel for one person to paddle
Qallunaaq (sing.) **Qallunaat (pl.)**	foreigners or strangers
Qaamaneq	glow of light; inner fire
Qaminngaarneq	the lights-out game, a sexual party game. Old custom where people had sex with strangers or other members of their settlement
Qilaat (sing.)	Greenlandic drum; used for entertainment in a musical or singing game, a singing duel, or for shamanism
Qilaneq	spirit fishing; a simple kind of shamanism that did not require much talent and could provide answers to basic yes/no questions
Qilertit	the traditional female topknot hairstyle
Qimarratit	scare spirit. Spirits called to terrify the audience during a shamanic event or ritual. Typically helper spirits could also act as scare spirits, but they could also be terrifying spirits such as *ANINGAAQ*
Sila	weather/mind/world. Religious conviction or spiritual view
Toornaq (sing.) **Toornat (pl.)**	helper spirit. Many different creatures could become helper spirits; they help an *angakkoq* during a spirit journey or shamanic ritual
Ulu (sing.) **Ulut (pl.)**	women's knife, used for flensing
Umiaq (sing.) **Umiat (pl.)**	a boat for wives and women. Large boat used to transport several people and equipment. The rowers were often women, led by a helmswoman

THE TEAM BEHIND THE BOOK

RESEARCH

MARIA BACH KREUTZMANN

Maria was born and bred in Nuuk and has been fascinated by monsters ever since she was a little girl. She has used Greenlandic mythology and all its colourful creatures in many of her personal projects and has long dreamt of sharing Greenlandic stories in a new and unique way.

She graduated from the Animation Workshop in Viborg, Denmark, in 2012, with a bachelor's degree in Computer Graphic Arts. Since then she has worked in the gaming and advertising industry in Denmark and the United Kingdom.

In January 2017, she moved back to Nuuk and has since worked on the Greenlandic film, culture, and literature scene as an illustrator and project manager with her company, Glaciem House.

UJAMMIUGAQ ENGELL

Ujammiugaq was born and bred in Nuuk, where she now lives with her family.

She spent some years in Denmark, where she studied History and Curating at the University of Copenhagen. Today she works as a communication manager at Greenland's National Museum and Archives.

Due to her Greenlandic-Danish background, Ujammiugaq has always had a particular interest in sagas and myths as well as the history of the Danish Commonwealth, which she works to share and promote every day.

ROBIN FENRIR MANSA HILLESTRØM

Robin was born and grew up in Nordsjælland, Denmark, but a series of unexpected events brought him ever closer to Greenland. He studied Culture and Modern History at the University of Greenland, Ilisimatusarfik, having previously studied History at the University of Copenhagen.

Robin lives in Nuuk, where he enjoys the weather and the wonderful view while he wonders how the past can be shared to make it relevant and help us better understand each other and the world around us.

QIVIOQ NIVI LØVSTRØM

Qivioq grew up in Nuuk and Ilulissat with stories about *SASSUMA ARNAA* and ghost stories about *IKUSIK*, the northern lights, and *QIVITTUT*.

Qivioq has previously studied Inuit Cultures, Arctic Archaeology, and History and Subject Didactics. She is currently studying Culture and Modern History at the University of Greenland, Ilisimatusarfik.

She still refuses to whistle at the northern lights.

ILLUSTRATIONS

AGUST KRISTINSSON

Agust is an Icelandic artist who graduated from the Animation Workshop in Viborg, Denmark, in 2012, with a bachelor's degree in Computer Graphic Arts. Since then he has worked in the gaming industry and has so far been art director on two games released on PlayStation and Xbox.

He has been freelance since 2017 and has added motion graphics to his skills—and has barely left his workstation ever since. From there he has worked on countless illustrations, a game, and various motion graphics projects.

CARINA LILLEGAARD LØVGREEN

Carina graduated with a bachelor's degree in Character Animation from the Animation Workshop in Viborg, Denmark, in 2012. Since 2014, she has worked as a Character Supervisor for the LEGO Ninjago TV series. Ever since childhood she has loved horses and the X-Men universe which, together with her degree, has made her the artist she is today. She has really enjoyed gaining an insight into traditional Greenlandic culture and drawing mythical creatures for this book.

CHRISTIAN FLEISCHER REX

Christian is a Greenlandic animator and illustrator who studied classic animation at the Animation Workshop in Viborg, Denmark. Christian has worked on several animated movies in Europe, including *Asterix and the Vikings*.

Today Christian lives in Nuuk, where he runs his own production company, Deluxus Studio. Here he produces animation, animated explainer videos, illustrations, and storyboards, and designs logos for businesses and organizations.

In 2008, Christian published the comic *Kaassassuk – The Orphan*, based on a Greenlandic story of the same name.

COCO APUNNGUAQ LYNGE

Coco Apunnguaq Lynge is an illustrator and visual artist. She specializes in drawing simple, beautiful, and colourful illustrations and characters. Throughout her childhood, she was fascinated by cartoons and design, which continue to provide her with inspiration and passion.

Coco was born in Nuuk, where she lived until she was five years old, after which she moved with her mother and younger sister to Denmark. She has always been proud of her Inuit heritage and was delighted when she was asked to illustrate the Greenlandic mythical creatures in this book.

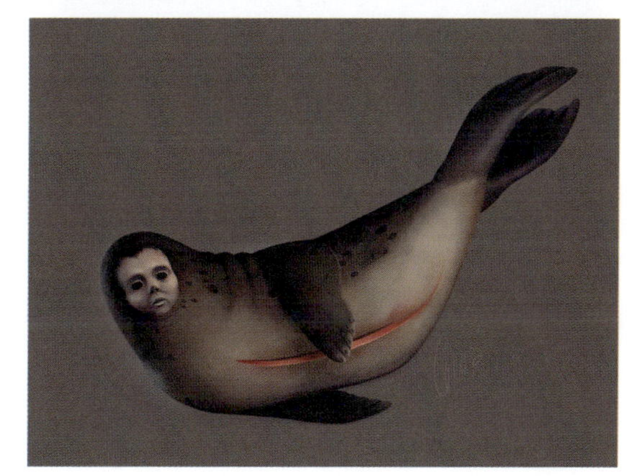
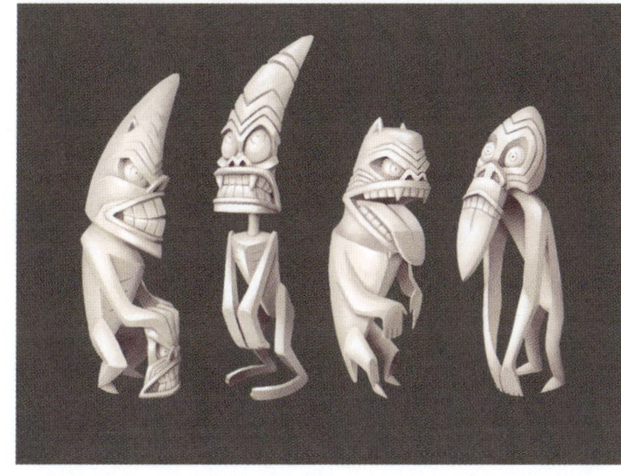

JONATAN BRÜSCH

Jonatan graduated from the Animation Workshop in 2012 with a bachelor's degree in Computer Graphic Arts. He has studied at several art colleges and has always been passionate about traditional and digital art.

Since finishing his studies, Jonatan has worked on everything from TV series to computer games in places such as Denmark, Germany, and Iceland.

He has really enjoyed this project and feels it has given him a better understanding and insight into Greenland's culture and history.

MAJA-LISA KEHLET

Maja-Lisa Kehlet was born and bred in Nuuk and grew up in a family where art and music were highly valued. She travelled to Denmark at the age of sixteen to continue her education and went on to study at the Animation Workshop, where she was awarded a bachelor's degree in Computer Graphic Arts in 2015. She has worked freelance on books, cover art, character designs, 3-D-based advertising, 3-D game development, 3-D backgrounds, and characters, and developed games. In 2018, she delivered a major illustration to PlayStation in connection with International Women's Day. She draws as much as she can in her spare time and is delighted that this guide will help highlight how much there is to discover in Greenlandic mythology.

In addition to these two full-page illustrations, Maria designed all vignettes/line art in the book.

MARTIN BRANDT HANSEN

Martin was born in Nuuk in 1990 and grew up in the suburb of Nuussuaq. After finishing school in Nuuk, he travelled to Denmark in 2013 to continue his studies. He has completed several creative courses, including at the Copenhagen School of Design, and he has worked with illustration in the world of media and children's literature. In 2016, he was accepted by Det Kongelige Danske Kunstakademis Billedkunstskoler, where he is studying for a bachelor's degree in Fine Arts.

BIBLIOGRAPHY

fra Kangeq, Aron, Arnaq Grove, Kirsten Thisted, and Gâba Thorning. *"Taama allattunga, Aron". Aalup Kangermiup oqaluttuai assilialiaalu tamakkiisut [1822-1869]*. Atuagaq 1, Nuuk: Atuakkiorfik, 1999.

——— *"Taama allattunga, Aron". Aalup Kangermiup oqaluttuai assilialiaalu tamakkiisut [1822-1869]*. Atuagaq 2, Nuuk: Atuakkiorfik, 1999.

fra Kangeq, Aron, and Kirsten Thisted. *"Således skriver jeg, Aron"– samlede fortællinger og illustrationer af Aron fra Kangeq [1822-1869]*. Bind 1, Nuuk: Atuakkiorfik, 1999.

——— *"Således skriver jeg, Aron"– samlede fortællinger og illustrationer af Aron fra Kangeq [1822-1869]*. Bind 2, Nuuk: Atuakkiorfik, 1999.

Bak, Ove. *Kujavarsiks rejse til månen: Eventyr fra Grønland.* København: Hernovs Forlag. 1977.

Bang, Kirsten: *Aandemaneren Maratse – og andre beretninger fra Angmagssalik.* København: Munksgaard, 1944.

Engelbrechtsen, Klaus, and Jørgen Thomsen. *Inuitisk religion og Mytologi.* Nuuk: Ilinniusiorfik Undervisningsmiddelforlag, 2013.

Holm, Gustav, and Hinrich Johannes Rink. *Sagn og Fortællinger fra Angmagsalik, Meddelelser om Grønland.* København: Reitzel, 1888.

Kreutzmann, Jens, and Kirsten Thisted. *Fortællinger og Akvareller.* Nuuk: Atuakkiorfik, 1997.

Holm, Gustav Frederik. *Ujuâts dagbøger fra Østgrønland, 1894-1935. Ved B. Rosenkilde Nielsen. Johan Petersens - Ujuâts - danske oversættelser. Østgrønlændernes sagn og fortælliger. Samlet af Gustav Holm i 1884-85. Påny udgivne ved William Thalbitzer.* Johan Christian August Petersen, and William Petersen, ed. København: Det Grønlandske Selskab, 1957.

Rasmussen, Knud. *500 leveregler, gamle ord og varsler fra Vestgrønland.* København: Det Grønlandske Selskab, 1979.

——— *Myter og Sagn fra Grønland, Bind I : Østgrønland.* Fredericia: Nordiske Landes Bogforlag, (1921) 1978.

——— *Myter og Sagn fra Grønland, Bind II : Vestgrønland.* Fredericia: Nordiske Landes Bogforlag, (1924) 1979.

——— *Myter og Sagn fra Grønland, Bind III : Kap York-distriktet og Nordgrønland.* Fredericia: Nordiske Landes Bogforlag, (1924) 1979.

Rasmussen, Knud, and Regitze Margrethe Søby. *Inuit Fortæller – Grønlandske Sagn og Myter, 1 : Frederikshåb, Julianehåb og Nanortalik.* Gjern: Bogans Forlag 1981.

——— *Inuit Fortæller – Grønlandske Sagn og Myter, 2 : Godthåb, Sukkertoppen, Holsteinsborg, Egedesminde og Upernavik.* Gjern: Bogans Forlag, 1981.

——— Inuit Fortæller – *Grønlandske Sagn og Myter, 3: Sydøstgrønland og Angmargssalik.* Gjern: Bogans Forlag, 1981.

Rink, Hinrich Johannes. *Eskimoiske Eventyr og Sagn – oversatte efter de indfødte Fortælleres Opskrifter og Meddelelser af H. Rink.* Kjøbenhavn: Rosenkilde og Bagger, (1866) 1982.

——— *Eskimoiske Eventyr og Sagn – indeholdende et Tillæg om Eskimoerne af H. Rink,* Supplement. Kjøbenhavn: Rosenkilde og Bagger 1982 (1871).

Rosing, Jens. *Sagn og Saga fra Angmagssalik, Rhodos 1984*
Sonne, Birgitte: Worldview of the Greenlanders – An Inuit Arctic Perspective. Fairbanks: University of Alaska Press, 2017.

Thalbitzer, William, and Gustav Holm, and Georg Amdrup. *The Ammassalik Eskimo: Contributions to the Ethnology of the East Greenland Natives Volume Part 2.* (København: Meddelelser om Grønland, 1941), 40:3.

Vebæk, Mâliâraq. *Tusarn! Sydgrønlandske fortællinger.* Nuuk: Atuakkiorfik, 2001.

Sonne Database

In addition to the works listed above, we have benefited enormously from the extensive Sonne Database, a comprehensive collection of sources and research on Greenlandic myths compiled over several decades by Birgitte Sonne. It is freely available to all on: www.arktiskinstitut.dk

Bestiarium Greenlandica:
a compendium of the mythical creatures, spirits, and strange beings of Greenland

First edition, *Bestiarium Groenlandica:* an illustrated guide
to the mythical creatures, spirits and animals of Greenland
published by milik publishing, 2018;
Second edition, *Bestiarium Greenlandica : a compendium of the mythical
creatures, spirits, and strange beings of Greenland*,
printed 2021 by Eye of Newt Books

Published by: Eye of Newt Books Inc. • www.eyeofnewtpress.com
Eye of Newt Books Inc., 56 Edith Drive,
Toronto, Ontario, M4R 1C3

Illustrated by: Coco Apunnguaq Lynge, Agust Kristinsson, Maja-Lisa Kehlet, Christian Fleischer Rex,
Jonatan Brüsch, Carina Lillegaard Løvgreen, Martin Brandt Hansen, Maria Bach Kreutzmann

ISBN: 978-1-7770817-0-6

Printed in China

www.eyeofnewtpress.com